Enlistment

PAUL BOUCHARD

A Novel

iUniverse, Inc.
New York Bloomington

Enlistment
A Novel

iUniverse books may be ordered through booksellers or by contacting:

iUniverse
1663 Liberty Drive
Bloomington, IN 47403
www.iuniverse.com
1-800-Authors (1-800-288-4677)

Because of the dynamic nature of the Internet, any Web addresses or links contained in this book may have changed since publication and may no longer be valid. The views expressed in this work are solely those of the author and do not necessarily reflect the views of the publisher, and the publisher hereby disclaims any responsibility for them.

The views expressed in Paul Bouchard's books are solely his own and are not affiliated with the United States army.

ISBN: 978-1-4502-4033-8 (sc)
ISBN: 978-1-4502-4034-5 (ebk)

Printed in the United States of America

iUniverse rev. date: 09/27/2012

For those who serve in the armed forces.

P.B.

El Paso, Texas
March 2010

Also by Paul Bouchard

A Package at GITMO

The Boy Who Wanted to Be a Man

ACKNOWLEDGMENTS

I couldn't have written this novel without assistance and support from the following people:

Army Sergeants Cade Loque and Curtis Vaughn, Army Captain Soren Seale, Marine Lieutenant Colonel (Ret.) Jay C. Smith, Army Specialists Thomas Redden and Austin Davidson, and Army Major (Ret.) Larry Winchel. Their insights on military training squared me away.

Army Sergeant David Irvin answered all my questions about the M16 weapon.

Terri Sirois, Ryan Little, Mark Whitcomb, Cory Kneeland, Racy Haddad, Jennifer Doak, Carla Arpa, Gerry Morin, John and Meena Allen, Brian Collin, Dave Howey, Brian Mathison, and Nevena and Brad Bentz. These are friends of mine who encouraged me to keep writing. Thanks guys.

Finally, special thanks to Robert Barnsby and Charles McElroy. Their critical eyes always make my manuscripts better.

A Note to the Reader

The Army, like the other military branches, has its own culture, terms, and vocabulary. So readers may better understand this novel, I've included a Glossary of Terms.

"Pain is good. Pain is just weakness leaving the body."

Drill Sergeant Murdock
addressing his new Basic
Training recruits, April 1994,
Fort Leonard Wood, Missouri

CHAPTER ONE

J ack Boudreau was sitting at a corner table on the first floor of Kansas City's sole Barnes & Noble bookstore. It was a sunny but cool Saturday afternoon in mid-November 1994. Boudreau, wearing a brown leather jacket, faded jeans, and a navy-blue sweatshirt, had four things on the small table in front of him: a paper cup—venti size—of Starbucks coffee, a half-eaten blueberry muffin on a glass plate, yesterday's copy of *The Wall Street Journal*, and a copy of Truman Capote's masterpiece *In Cold Blood*. The time was just minutes shy of one o'clock in the afternoon.

Boudreau, age twenty six, was an Army journalist stationed at nearby Fort Leavenworth. On weekends, it was his practice to frequent that Barnes & Noble bookstore because it was his favorite place to work on the novel he was beginning to write. He had written the novel's prologue, and he was working on a detailed plot outline.

But this particular Saturday afternoon was different for Boudreau and a departure from his regular practice and routine. He was having his favorite snack (the blueberry muffin), and he was sipping from an ever-present cup of coffee — he consumed five to eight cups daily. But Boudreau wasn't working on the novel that afternoon—not after what had happened earlier that week. Carlos, a fellow Fort Leavenworth soldier, had swung by Boudreau's place of employment, Fort Leavenworth's Public Affairs Office, the day before and had made it clear he wanted to meet with and talk to Boudreau man-to-man, one-on-one. Boudreau had suggested they meet Saturday at the Barnes & Noble bookstore in Kansas City's Plaza section. They settled on four PM as a meeting time.

I don't want to work on the novel this afternoon, Boudreau thought as he sipped some coffee. *I need to clear my head and think about this past week. I'm way early for this four PM meeting with Carlos, and that gives me plenty of time to figure it out. Besides, I want to read* The Wall Street Journal *and get back to* In Cold Blood.

Boudreau interlaced his hands and placed them behind his head. He leaned back in his chair and looked through the large picture windows in front of him. His mind was busy and immune to the surrounding patron traffic and chatter.

Well, I know the gist of what Carlos wants to talk about. I've sure got lots of questions for him though. I know "The Boys" were involved.

He slowly leaned forward and took a bite of muffin.

But some of the things Carlos said to me yesterday— hmm?—that's where I've got lots of questions for him. What did he mean?

"We would've gotten you, J.B, 'cause our plan was perfect— you'd have been kicked out of the Army. Back to Fort Living Room as a civilian is where you was headin', bro. Something gave you away, J.B."

And something about, "Our bad luck was your good luck, Jack."

Well, I've got questions for him. I especially want to know about the plan that supposedly would have gotten me kicked out of the Army.

Boudreau took a quick sip of coffee, and then he started reading *The Wall Street Journal.* The answers to his many questions would come in three hours.

CHAPTER TWO

It wasn't supposed to be this way, at least not in his mind, because he had had plans—plans of being a big-time reporter or columnist like a David Broder or a Robert Novak. Or maybe going on to law school and becoming a lawyer. That too had been in the plans.

Lawyer—nice everything: nice suits, nice shirts, nice car, a nice home in the nicer neighborhoods. A nice girlfriend-turned wife down the road. Nice.

Those had been his dreams, and he hadn't given up on them yet, but they were on hold—on the backburner for now—because Jack Boudreau, a struggling stringer reporter out of Bangor, Maine, had, in the spring of 1994, enlisted in the Army. No, it wasn't supposed to be this way.

Instead of working as a journalist or studying law, he had found himself standing inside the cramped middle section of a cattle truck with the other forty members of his platoon in the truck, wearing military fatigues. Two large Army duffle bags, placed upright and vertical, hugged his sides for the thirty-minute, cattle-truck drive to a Fort Leonard Wood, Missouri, Basic Training site.

Never thought I'd be one to join the military, he thought. *It wasn't supposed to be this way.*

* * *

It wasn't supposed to be this way because Jack Boudreau had graduated from college four years prior with a degree in journalism and a minor in political science. He had, by all accounts, done everything right—good grades, the right internships, solid networking. But upon graduation he found himself jobless, and it took him six months—six long months of hitting the job-search pavement with tons of resumes and writing samples—to finally land one job offer as a stringer for the *Bangor Daily News*. No paid vacations, no health insurance or a dental plan, no pension plan either, and "we pay by the word count with the understanding we will edit and often cut your articles." Running out of money—borrowed money at that—Boudreau took the stringer job.

One year went by, a year of many articles: articles on the University of Maine Black Bears baseball team returning to the College World Series; the eighty-nine-year-old great grandmother who won the blueberry-pie baking contest at the Brewer City Fair; coverage of the Potato Blossom Festival in Fort Fairfield; a spread about an economic summit in Rockland; a feature on a local artist in Bar Harbor; an interview with a self-made trucking magnate out of Houlton; countless traffic accidents; more town-hall meetings than he could remember; a feature on Maine's annual moose hunt. Many, many articles, often four or five per week—more than two hundred in all. And Boudreau made just barely over fifteen thousand dollars before taxes that first year.

Still, the dream—the plan of being a big-time reporter or columnist—had still been alive and well.

Then came year two. It was a repeat of year one with two exceptions—a slight pay raise, $16,200 before Uncle Sam's take, and the start of sending writing samples to bigger news markets like Portland, Manchester, Hartford, and Boston, all in the hopes of landing a better journalism job with better pay.

Then came year three—a repeat of years one and two: many articles, enjoying the work, but dirt poor. And no calls from Portland or the other bigger media markets.

It was in that third year with the *Bangor Daily News* that Boudreau took an afternoon trip to Bangor's sole shopping mall. There was nothing unusual about the trip — Boudreau visited the shopping mall maybe twice a month to check out the latest in books, movies, or music. But on that particular mall visit Boudreau noticed a small metal stand situated next to the mall's main entrance. The stand was fitted with Army recruiting brochures. Curious, Boudreau picked up a brochure and read it.

The chance to serve your nation.

The possibility of Officer Candidate School.

Money for college in the form of the G.I. Bill.

Many job opportunities—mechanics, truck drivers, infantry, cooks, computer technicians, journalists.

What the heck, he thought. *I'll keep my options open. I'll keep a brochure.*

* * *

Less than six weeks after picking up that Army recruiting brochure, Boudreau's boss, a forty-two-year-old managing editor by the name of Brian Reynolds, called his favorite stringer to his office.

"J.B., have a seat. Coffee?"

"Nah, boss, I've already had my quota for the day," replied Boudreau. He took a seat across the desk from Reynolds.

He thought, *This can't be good—Reynolds never calls me to his office.*

Reynolds got right to the point.

"Jack, I'm afraid I've got some bad news. You know this computer thing, this information-age crap, is really cutting into our industry. Our revenue stream just ain't what it used to be. You know I like you, and it's nothing personal, but we just can't afford to run all your stories. Paper's cutting back, Jack. You still have a job with us, but we'll only take two, maybe three, articles from you each week. And no sports—we're consolidating the sports section."

Calm, but frustrated and a bit nervous, Boudreau managed a weak reply, "I understand."

* * *

Ten minutes after Reynolds's delivery of the bad news, Boudreau was in his car heading to his apartment. It was a cold and wet afternoon, and Boudreau's car—a 1979 Volvo sedan with more than three-hundred-thousand miles—was fogging up from the inside, the result of a faulty defroster.

Christ, he thought as he exited off a service road. *A work cutback. I'm already struggling; now I'm even poorer. I drive a crummy old rust bucket; I have the tiniest of studio apartments; I live in the crummy part of town; and now a work cutback. What will Cindy think?*

* * *

"With your college degree you'd start off as a specialist, Mr. Boudreau."

That's what the Army recruiter told Boudreau two days after Reynolds's fateful "cutbacks" talk. Boudreau, sitting in the recruiter's office, was all ears. He caught a glimpse of the recruiter's nametag. It read "Peterson."

"With your ABSVAB scores you get to pick your career field," Peterson said.

Boudreau had taken the ABSVAB (the Armed Services Vocational Aptitude Battery test) "just for fun" three weeks prior.

"Full health and dental coverage of course. Thirty days paid vacation—we call vacation time 'leave' in the Army. And with your college degree, I'd say your best bet would be to enlist, do a year or two, make sergeant, then submit a packet for OCS—Officer Candidate School."

"And I'd get the G.I. Bill. Right?" asked Boudreau.

"Yes, absolutely," said Peterson. "Here's how it works: We'd take a hundred dollars out of your paycheck every month for twelve months. That's twelve-hundred dollars, but in return we give you more than twenty-five thousand for college. For you, that could be graduate school or law school—you told me you're thinking of law school, right?"

"Yes I am, sir" said Boudreau.

"That's great. Army has its own lawyers you know. JAG Corps is always recruiting, too. You know, Mr. Boudreau, there's plenty of lawyer jokes out there, but we sure need them lawyers don't we? I got me a fine Army JAG Officer when I got in a pickle back when I was a drill sergeant. Female recruit accused me of harassment. It was all bullshit, of course. JAG Officer saved me a stripe and my career. Anyway, I'm getting off track. How does this all sound—pick your Army job, benefits, G.I. Bill?"

"Sounds great," replied Boudreau.

Then he asked, "Uh, Mr. Peterson, how much does an Army specialist make? How much does it pay?"

"Good question. Let's see." Peterson pulled out a desk drawer. "Okay, give me a sec here." He was looking at a sheet. "I have here the 1993 pay charts. Specialist—that's an E-4. Oh, then there's your BAQ and BAS—your basic allowance for quarters and subsistence. Oh, but you're not married right?"

"Well, I'm pretty serious with my girlfriend and—"

"Oh yeah," said Peterson, cutting him off. "You already told me that—girlfriend. Well, you'd be making twenty-one thousand if you lived in the barracks or if you lived in free government housing. You can't be shacking up though, if you want that free government housing; you gotta tie the knot for that. Otherwise you're in the barracks. Barracks is free just like post housing."

Boudreau said nothing.

Peterson cleared his throat. "Uh, you'd make twenty-eight thousand if you qualify for the BAQ. That's the Army paying you to live off-base either because there's no post housing available or you're on the housing waiting list. You need to be married, too, for that BAQ. Some installations give BAQ to single soldiers, but that's usually for E-5s and above. E-5's a sergeant, one rank above your specialist rank."

Boudreau was absorbing it all. He didn't sign up right then and there, but the seed of enlisting in the Army had been planted.

* * *

A month passed. Same stringer job, just fewer beats and fewer articles to write, which meant less money, which meant the necessity of getting a second job to make ends meet. For Boudreau, the moonlighting job came in the form of delivering pizzas for a local Dominoes Pizza franchise, and his life became: the same crummy apartment; the same rust bucket for a car; no calls from the bigger newspapers; and an on-again-off-again relationship with a UMaine graduate student in English named Cindy Jones, who was an intern at the *Bangor Daily News.* Boudreau had met her ten months prior, and now that he was moonlighting, he was seeing less of her.

Two months passed.

Boudreau thought, *I'm giving myself another month. If I don't hear anything from another newspaper—if I don't get an offer for a job— then I'll enlist in the Army. Cindy seems supportive enough. Sure, I'd do the grad school thing or law school thing right now if I could swing it financially, but those options mean more student loans and I'm already pretty deep in student loan debt. Army's the best thing for me, man— better pay, benefits, and, most importantly, money in the form of the G.I. Bill. Besides, I'm in decent shape. Heck, I jog five miles almost every day. Plus, I get to choose my military job. I'd choose journalism, of course. I'll make it in the Army; I know I'll make it. An Army reporter. That could work.*

A month later and still with no new job offers, Boudreau, true to his plan, visited Recruiter Peterson and signed the necessary paperwork to enlist in the Army. Soon thereafter, he submitted his resignation to the *Bangor Daily News,* left his pizza delivery job, and was the recipient of a beer-and-music-filled farewell party, courtesy of family and friends.

* * *

Later that same evening, after both she and Jack had sobered from the farewell party, Cindy insisted she drive Jack back to his apartment. Jack agreed.

"Listen, Jack. I love you," Cindy said as she took the wheel of the old Volvo. "I know I moved out of your apartment two months ago, but that was just to get 'my space' and to 'think hard' about things. I love you, Jack. Show me you love me. You'll be gone for awhile because of your Army training. Show me you love me, Jack. Show me you're committed to me and to us. Show me you love me, Jack, with a diamond engagement ring."

Two days later, Boudreau bought a twelve-hundred-dollar engagement ring, courtesy of VISA plastic, and Cindy moved back into the crummy studio apartment. Seventeen days after that, Jack Boudreau, age twenty six, was wearing military fatigues and was crowded into the cattle truck on the way to Fort Leonard Wood, Missouri.

It wasn't supposed to be this way.

CHAPTER THREE

While Boudreau was about to start his eight-week-long Basic Training, Specialist Dustin Boros, a three-year Army veteran, was getting ready to PCS (permanent change of station) from Fort Campbell, Kentucky, to Fort Leavenworth, Kansas. Boros, an Army supply clerk, had spent two years at Fort Campbell—home of the famed 101st Airborne Division—and while stationed there, he learned just how profitable the illegal marijuana trade could be.

Boros's mentor at Campbell was a Clarksville, Tennessee, based drug dealer (most of Fort Campbell was in the state of Tennessee), and Boros learned all there was to learn about pricing, drug supply networks, pot plants and how to plant them, security, and communications. Now, with his upcoming PCS move to Fort Leavenworth, Boros was confident the drug-trade knowledge he had acquired at Fort Campbell would serve him well in Kansas, especially since he had plans of striking out on his own and of running his own drug-trafficking outfit.

Boros, of course, had never heard of Jack Boudreau, and neither had Boudreau ever heard of Dustin Boros.

CHAPTER FOUR

Crowded and cramped on the cattle truck. April of 1994. Fort Leonard Wood, Missouri.

Boudreau, like the other young men on board the cattle truck, was wearing military fatigues.

Six days prior, Boudreau had flown from Bangor to St. Louis by way of Baltimore, and then he had hopped onto a chartered bus to reach Fort Leonard Wood. Upon arrival, Boudreau's head was shaved, and he was issued his gear: four sets of military fatigues, otherwise called battle dress uniforms or BDUs; two pairs of Army boots; six pairs of Army socks; two soft caps; two Army duffle bags; three Army PT (physical training) uniforms; and a thick, compact Basic Training book called the SMART book, which covered everything a recruit needed to know about Basic Training. After that came five days of instruction, and that's where Boudreau, like the other Army recruits, learned how to march, how to salute, how to polish boots, and how to properly make a bunk bed. Those five days were otherwise known as inprocessing week.

"Recruits, pack all your shit into your duffle bags," came the order from one of the inprocessing sergeants at the end of Day Five.

"After your stuff's packed up, line up outside in a line—we have to see if you guys can do ten push-ups. After you do your ten push-ups, then line up, by platoon, next to a cattle truck.

If you can't do ten push-ups then your sorry ass will stay back here for another week until you can do ten push-ups."

The inprocessing sergeant ended with, "Recruits, this ain't no time for any of you to be a fucking pussy. Don't be a sissy; don't be a wuss. Do your fucking ten push-ups, hop on a cattle truck, and start your Basic Training. You guys make it through this little push-up thing and y'all be assigned to your Basic Training Company, C-4-10. That's Charlie Company. I think the 4-10 stands for Fourth Battalion, Tenth Infantry. Good luck, and remember—don't be a wuss."

After doing his push-ups, Boudreau crowded onto the cramped cattle truck. He knew he was going to be a member of First Platoon, C-4-10. He also knew two other platoons made up C-4-10, but he didn't know any of the recruits from Second or Third Platoon. He did know a few of his fellow First Platooners from the just-completed inprocessing week:

Alvarez, a short, dark-haired Hispanic from Los Angeles.

Bodin, a slim six-footer from the Boston area.

Carrington, a blondish-haired, thick-frame country boy from Louisiana. Boudreau figured Carrington must have been a wrestler at some point because he had cauliflower ears.

Carey, a short, skinny eighteen-year-old who barely passed the recent push-up test.

Brown, a short, pudgy black guy from Alabama.

Cassell, a rugged, mustachioed country boy from New Hampshire.

Bodette, a tall, broad-shouldered twenty-two-year-old from the suburbs of Atlanta.

Boudreau, like most of the recruits, remained silent while on the cattle truck. He kept both his hands firmly gripped on each fully-filled duffle bag. His thoughts kept shifting—

I hope Cindy's okay ...

I think I'll be all right with this Basic Training thing. Running, push-ups, sit-ups, marching, taking orders. I'll be okay ...

I'm actually anxious to start work as an Army reporter. Maybe me and Cindy should get married right after Basic

Training...no, after AIT (advanced individual training). My AIT's the military journalism school. I'm looking forward to that training ...

Yeah, after AIT, we get married. Hopefully, I'll come up on orders to Germany. Cindy always wanted to see Europe. Me too ...

Later on, I can use my G.I. Bill to help pay for law school ...

Hope the old Volvo doesn't break down ...

I hope Cindy's okay ...

A sudden stop. The sound of the cattle truck's air pressure brakes releasing air. The slide door opens.

"Move out! Move out! You shit-for-brain recruits have thirty seconds to get off that cattle truck. Thirty, twenty-nine, twenty-eight ..."

CHAPTER FIVE

Soon after PCSing to Fort Leavenworth, Specialist Boros started driving around the countryside surrounding the military base. Whether he was in Kansas or nearby Missouri, Boros was looking for rarely visited land that was fertile and suitable to grow his illegal cash crop. He was also making plans and contacts with marijuana dealers in Kentucky, Virginia, and far-away British Columbia, Canada, to supply him with his initial stock of product.

Boros had all the qualities of a successful entrepreneur: patience, drive, vision, focus, the willingness to take risks, an eye for talent when he saw it, a constant eye on the ball and an ear to the ground, the ability to schmooze and sell, and perhaps the most important quality of all—*no feelings*.

"Bizness is bizness" was not only a popular saying for Boros, it was something he believed in, something he lived by. *Need to cut costs— cut costs; need to fire some dude—fire his ass.* "Bizness is bizness." *No feelings.*

It took Boros no more than a week to find six parcels of suitable land for marijuana growing—four parcels in Kansas, two parcels in Missouri. Then, after the land selection, came the need to recruit help to help him build his startup criminal enterprise. To do that, Boros started hitting bars and clubs on Thursday, Friday, and Saturday nights in the hope of networking and getting to know drug dealers and anyone who might be interested in working for his outfit. A few names popped up, but no one panned out. By then, however, Boros had one particular fellow in mind, Army Specialist Pernell Jackson.

Always wanted someone on the inside, Boros thought, and Jackson was, of all things, an Army MP stationed at Fort Leavenworth.

Corrupt Military Policeman. That's what I need. That's what Sergeant Kemper had at Fort Campbell—he had an MP on the take and it worked beautifully for him. Plus, word is Jackson ain't exactly a choir boy. Plus, he needs money.

And so it was. On a particular Friday night, Boros made it a point to sit next to Jackson at a local club, and in no time he waved at one of the cocktail waitresses.

"Waitress, how 'bout another round of beer for my Army buddy here? Jackson, isn't it?"

CHAPTER SIX

"**M**ove out! Move out! You shit-for-brain recruits have thirty seconds to get off that cattle truck. Thirty, twenty-nine, twenty-eight ..."

Boudreau's heart jumped. He noticed recruits pushing and shoving each other, all in an effort to exit the cattle truck in the allotted time.

He heard, "Move, move motherfucker," and "hurry up" behind him, but he couldn't move because he was boxed in by other recruits.

"Nineteen, eighteen ..."

Boudreau kept inching up toward the truck opening. There was more pushing and shoving. He was holding on firmly to his two duffle bags.

"Twelve, eleven, ten ..."

Some clearing. More movement towards the exit. Boudreau figured maybe half the recruits had exited the truck.

"Six, five, four ..."

Boudreau exited the cattle truck and quickly walked down a wide and sturdy metal ramp.

"*Whew. Made it,* he thought. He immediately saw dark threatening clouds coming from the west, and he guessed the temperature to be in the mid-sixties.

"Three, two, one. Time! Okay, you sorry pukes didn't make it," one of the drill sergeants yelled at the recruits who were still in the cattle truck. Boudreau, now standing in formation on a grass field with the other First Platooners who had made it off the truck in time, counted eight drill sergeants—seven around the large grass field and one next to the cattle truck he had just exited. The drill sergeants were easy to recognize because they wore distinctive drill-sergeant felt hats, hats that resembled those worn by U.S. Park Service rangers.

"Well, all righty now," said the drill sergeant closest to the cattle truck. "Well, well, well. So you sorry asses didn't make the countdown, huh? Well, hurry up. Hurry up and move out of that cattle truck now and get your sorry asses with your battle buddies over there in that formation."

The recruits in the cattle truck did as ordered, and in less than a minute, all of First Platoon was formed up on the large grass field. Boudreau, his two duffle bags still to his side, noticed two more cattle trucks pulling alongside the curb.

Recruits from Second and Third Platoon, he thought.

"Well, well, well—not all of you boys made the countdown," said the drill sergeant who stood at the head of the formation. It was the same drill sergeant who had just stood next to the cattle truck. "And I can say 'boys' because I don't see any chicks amongst y'all. An all-male company. Cute. That's just the way I like it. Army should be all-male in my opinion, but that ain't my fuckin' call to make. That's way above my pay grade, and that's a call for Slick Willy to make—a fuckin' draft dodger, mind ya. Anyway, ain't no chicks here, but we do have two female drill sergeants for this here First Platoon—Staff Sergeant Hudnall and Staff Sergeant Ferro. They both can kick any of y'all's asses so treat 'em with proper respect. And forget that shit I just told y'all 'bout the Army should be all-male. I'll make an exception for Staff Sergeants Hudnall and Ferro. I wouldn't mind having any one of them in my foxhole if shit hits the fan and the bullets start flying."

The recruits, all at the position of attention, said nothing. Boudreau, who was standing in the second row of the platoon, was able to catch a glimpse of the drill sergeant's name tag. It read "Murdock."

I'm guessing Murdock's probably six-foot-two and 220 pounds, he thought. *Man, he's got big forearms. Huge forearms. Popeye forearms.*

"At ease," ordered Murdock, and the recruits instinctively came to the position of at ease. Murdock started pacing around the platoon.

"Now since some of you bunch of shits didn't make the time limit, y'all are gonna do some push-ups. See pukes, there's something y'all better start understanding, and the quicker y'all do the better. See, y'all ain't alone no more. You gotta think of your unit, your company, and your battle buddy," Murdock said loudly.

He stopped pacing around the platoon.

"Some of you shits made the time limit, but not all of ya. So, in proper military fashion, y'all are gonna pay the price for not completing the task as a platoon. That means push-ups, pukes."

There was a pause.

"Well just don't stand there pukes—start pushing!" Murdock exclaimed at the top of his lungs. "Push-up pukes! Now!"

Every First Platoon C-4-10 recruit hit the ground and started doing push-ups.

"Remember pukes, there ain't no individuals here," Murdock said as he resumed pacing around the platoon. The other drill sergeants also started pacing around the recruits.

"Ain't no heroes amongst y'all. Y'all just keep finding that real estate—keep pushing out those push-ups, and start thinking and executing like a team, like a platoon. Lemme tell y'all something. I'm a native Missourian. That's right—this is my home state, and y'all know what they call Missoura, right?"

He pronounced Missouri "Missour-rah."

"It's the Show Me state. Y'all need to show me something."

The recruits kept doing push-ups.

Murdock continued. "And lemme tell y'all another thing, pukes. If you're looking for sympathy, your sorry ass has come to the wrong fuckin' place. You're not on the block anymore. You want sympathy, look in *Webster's Dictionary* between shit and syphilis—that's where y'all fuckin' find sympathy. Not here pukes. Not in my platoon."

The recruits kept doing push-ups. Moans and heavy breathing could be heard. Boudreau, who thought he was in decent shape, felt his upper arms tightening up.

"Oh, some of you—in fact most of you—are hurting huh?" said Murdock with a grin on his face. He suddenly stopped pacing, crossed his big arms, looked down on the ground, and spat tobacco juice on the grass.

"Pukes," he said, "just remember this: pain is good. Pain is just weakness leaving the body."

CHAPTER SEVEN

Boudreau leaned back in his chair and took another small bite from his blueberry muffin. He had just finished reading *The Wall Street Journal.* He glanced at his watch. It read one thirty in the afternoon.

He thought: *Well, I'm looking forward to reading Capote's book for the second time, but before starting, I need to think about meeting Carlos.*

He took a sip of coffee.

Man, I'm guessing The Boys knew I knew something about their planned shooting at the Taco Bell. And now Carlos wants to talk. Hmm, he thought. *I'm hoping Carlos will answer my questions.*

Boudreau took another sip of coffee. He noticed more patrons entering the Barnes & Noble bookstore.

Hmm—yesterday Carlos said 'We would have gotten you, J.B. Our plan was perfect.' And something about getting me kicked out of the Army.

Boudreau reached for his muffin.

I figured The Boys were on my tail and following my trail, but what was their plan? Their so-called perfect plan? Something about back to Fort Living Room as a civilian is where you would have gone. And Carlos had said "our bad luck was your good luck."

Hmm? wondered Boudreau. *Carlos will be here in two-and-a-half hours. I hope I get answers to my questions.*

He again leaned back in his chair, and then he gently shook his venti paper cup.

I'm running low on the go-go juice. I'll get myself another coffee before I start reading In Cold Blood.

CHAPTER EIGHT

F ive more minutes of push-ups. Boudreau, with his hands, chest, and the front of his thighs hugging the grass, saw a few tiny raindrops land on his left index finger. An intermittent drizzling rain ensued.

"All right, privates—get up! Get up!" barked Murdock. "Y'all stop doing push-ups and get in line behind one of those orange coolers behind you and get your sorry asses some water to drink. Move! Y'all got five mikes to drink some water; five minutes! And I'm starting the clock now!"

The C-4-10 First Platoon recruits got up and hurriedly did as ordered.

"No seconds now," yelled one of the drill sergeants. "Just one drink per puke. Pick up one white foam cup, fill it up with water, drink the cup, then toss your cup in the black plastic bag next to the cooler. Keep the line moving."

Each recruit drank a cup of water and was back in formation within the five-minute time limit. Boudreau, feeling okay even though his chest and triceps were burning from all those push-ups, stood at the position of at ease next to his two duffle bags. Suddenly, from the corner of his left eye, he noticed a tall and heavy-set recruit collapse and fall to the ground. He heard a soft "thump" as the big recruit's backside hit the ground. One of the drill sergeants rushed to the fallen recruit.

"You two," said the drill sergeant who was helping the recruit to his feet. He pointed at two recruits standing in the

First Squad of First Platoon. "You two recruits help me get this fat-fuck-tub-of-shit in the shade."

The two selected recruits followed the order and helped bring the fallen recruit under the shade of a nearby oak tree.

"Well, well, well, pukes, welcome to Fort Leonard Wood, Missourah," Murdock said loudly as he stood in front of First Platoon. "And don't none of you worry 'bout that fat boy who just gave himself a wake-up call. He's a big boy, he'll be okay." Murdock again spat some tobacco juice on the grass in front of him.

"Well, this here Fort Leonard Wood is otherwise known as Fort Lost In The Woods," said Murdock. "As y'all can see there's plenty of trees and forest here, and it's fairly easy to get lost in 'em, thus the name."

Murdock started pacing around the formation.

"How those push-ups feel, pukes? Good I hope. Y'all be doing lots of push-ups here, so y'all better get used to the feeling."

He stopped pacing, and he crossed his thick arms over his chest.

"Well little 'bout myself, pukes. I'm a graduate of John Wayne University. Now I know some of you pukes are college boys, but you've probably never heard of John Wayne University. At John Wayne University, I got my degree in shooting down targets. What am I telling you sorry asses? I'm telling you the Army is what I am and who I am. It's all that I know. John Wayne University, pukes—that's Uncle Sam's Army. That's where I went to school."

Murphy again spat some tobacco juice on the grass.

"I've been in Uncle Sam's great Army for fifteen years. By the way, any of you pukes know what U.S. Army stands for? Lemme say those letters slowly for y'all: U-S-A-R-M-Y."

The recruits remained silent and at the position of at ease.

"Lemme help y'all out," said Murdock. "It stands for Uncle Sam Ain't Released Me Yet. That's right—I ain't been released yet, pukes. Yep, fifteen years. I've been in this Army fifteen years, and I'm here for the long haul. Shit, fifteen years into something, I might as well tough it out another five years and get me a pension, right?"

None of the recruits said a thing.

"Hell, I ain't got no beef with Uncle Sam's Army," continued Murdock. "Shit y'all, I've been sucking on the big government military tit for fifteen years, so I might as well suck on that big one some more, right? Shit, five more years to go, pukes. Five more years and then I can go on KMB duty. Anyone of you know what KMB duty is? Anyone? Maybe some of you college boys know what KMB duty is. Anyone?"

No one spoke.

"Stands for Kiss My Butt Duty. That's right. Once I'm retired, y'all can kiss my butt, but until then y'all better listen to what me and the other drill sergeants have to say."

Murdock again spat tobacco juice on the ground.

"Now pukes, do y'all know what U.S. Army stands for in reverse? In case y'all are wondering, that's Y-M-R-A-S-U." He pronounced each letter slowly and loudly.

"Anyone?"

Again no one spoke.

"Stands for Yes My Retarded Ass Signed Up. That's you, pukes—that's you guys. Shit, now that we're on this topic, I want to personally thank each and every one of you pukes for enlisting in Uncle Sam's Army. Join the Army—heh—that's good shit right there. The juice is worth the squeeze. We're gonna have ourselves a party here for the next eight weeks."

Murphy resumed pacing. He was heading toward the Second Platoon recruits.

"All righty then. Lemme start off by saying that the best advice I have for y'all is to follow orders. Just follow our orders, and ain't none of y'all will have a problem. Don't be a knucklehead. Don't be ate up like a fuckin' soup sandwich. Whatever you do, don't make it a goat rope—do it well; do it the right way. One thing to remember about the Army is failure ain't an option. Work hard. Don't give up. Don't quit. If obstacles come your way—fuck it; suck it up and drive on. Complete the mission, pukes. Don't ever get lost in the sauce. Just follow orders, pukes. Follow orders, get with the fuckin' program, drink the fuckin' Kool Aid, and don't screw the pooch. If we tell you to drink the fuckin' Kool Aid, then drink the fuckin' Kool Aid. If we tell y'all to zig, then don't be fuckin' zagging; fuckin' zig. It's time y'all get in Nike mode—Just Fuckin' Do It. The sooner y'all get with the program, the better. Just work hard, and bust a nut for us. I know it's tough to push the noodle up the flagpole, but sometimes that's what y'all gotta do."

Murdock stopped pacing. He started scanning the entire three-platoon, C-4-10 company.

"Now, coupla things to cover, pukes. One—this ain't no Burger King; you can't have it your way, pukes. It's Uncle Sam's way now. Just follow orders, and none of you will have problems. Follow orders, pukes. I don't wanna see any of you sorry-ass pukes eat a retard sandwich, okay? Basic Training ain't no time to get creative and start questioning shit. So, this ain't no Burger King, pukes, and you can't have it your way—it's Uncle Sam's way now, but don't none of you worry. We'll give y'all three hots and a cot. That's three hot meals and a cot for those of you who are a little slow on the uptake. Actually, y'all have your own bunk bed, and y'all get a sleeping bag when we're out in the field. Now that ain't that bad, is it?"

The recruits remained quiet. Boudreau, still at the position of at ease, started rolling his feet slowly. *That's what the instructors told us during inprocessing week,* he thought. *Bend your knees a bit, and roll off your feet some. That's how you prevent locking your knees and fainting. That big recruit probably just locked his knees; that's why he passed out momentarily.*

"And we'll also give you time to worship," said Murdock, still eyeing the recruits. "I don't give a fuck who y'all's God is or isn't. Me, well I'm partial to the Jewish carpenter. Last name's Christ, first name's Jesus. He's my big boss, but I don't give a rat's ass if y'all are a Jew, or a Muslim, or a Hindu, or a peaceful Buddhist—whatever. Actually, on that peaceful Buddhist shit, I think that's the problem with being soft, with being too peaceful. Mother-fucking Commy Chinese run over your ass and take over your country. But anyway, I digress a bit. Bottom line, pukes, we'll give y'all time on Sundays to worship. So that ain't so bad, huh—three meals, a place to sleep, some time to worship. Everybody tracking?"

"Hooah," replied the recruits in unison, confirming they understood.

"Good, good," said Murdock. He resumed pacing.

"Now everybody understand this ain't no Burger King, right?"

The recruits remained quiet.

"Everybody understand it's the Army way now, and not y'all's way, right? How 'bout some north-south action on that Burger King stuff. C'mon Charlie-4-10, y'all know what north-south means—not east-west now, I want some north-south action on that question. I know the sergeants over at inprocessing showed y'all the ropes. C'mon now, give me a north-south approval nod on that Burger Kind shit."

All the recruits nodded their heads in the north-south, up-and-down direction as a sign of approval.

Murdock stopped pacing. "That's good, pukes. Real good. I know y'all are jacked up, but I also know y'all had one week of inprocessing, so this can't be too bad of a cluster fuck. Anyway, Burger King's a No Go right? Y'all gimme an east-west nodding 'bout that Burger King crap. Go on now, gimme an east-west for Burger King."

All the C-4-10 recruits, as ordered, shook their heads in the east-west, left-to-right direction, a sign of disapproval.

"Good, good," said Murdock. "Real good. Okay, second thing: at no time will any of you sorry asses ever take a taxi cab or go to the PX Post Exchange Store or drink caffeinated products or eat sweets and desserts. No taxis, no PX, no caffeine products—that's not just coffee and tea, it also includes sodas. Desserts too—they's also a No Go. If y'all perform well during Basic then maybe us high-speed drill sergeants will loosen up a bit on your sorry asses, but for now, none of that shit. Tracking? Gimme a north-south on that one too, Charlie-4-10."

The recruits nodded their heads from north to south as a sign of approval. Boudreau, as he was nodding, thought: *Sure glad I quit my coffee habit last week. I had headaches for three days, but then they went away. I feel fine now.*

"Third thing," said Murdock. He was now standing in front of Second Platoon. "Third thing is that at no time will any of you shit-for-brains smoke or use tobacco products. That includes chewing tobacco." Murdock paused for just a second or two, then he smiled.

"Now, as I'm sure some of y'all have noticed, yours truly here is currently chewing some fine-ass tobacco. That's right, I am chewing tobacco. But guess what, pukes—I can. Shit, fifteen years in the Army and good old Uncle Sugar will give you a little Burger King. He'll let you have it your way a bit. Fact is pukes I ain't no recruit like you sorry asses are. I did my Basic long back. Y'all need this school, but I don't. Shit, y'all, I've served my country for fifteen years. Got me a Bronze Star too in that little conflict we had not too long ago—that little conflict in the Big Sandbox called Iraq. Personally, I think we didn't fully complete the mission on that one. We should've gone after Hussein's ass and whupped his butt real good.

"Anyway, I'm getting off track here. Point is pukes, I ain't no recruit. We drill sergeants can smoke and drink coffee, but your sorry asses can't right now. Clear? Everybody tracking? Gimme a north-south 'bout that tobacco shit."

The C-4-10 recruits nodded in approval.

"Good. That's good," said Murdock. He once again spat tobacco juice on the ground.

"Four—no porn. I, or any of the drill sergeants, better not find any fuck magazines in your wall lockers or rucksacks. That's contraband, pukes. Just like switchblades and shit—they's contraband, too. Now I know y'all had a shakedown inspection during inspection week, so that means none of you have any contraband. That's good; let's keep it that way. No porn, pukes. Y'all probably have little dicks anyway so it shouldn't be a big issue. Find some other fuckin' way to get a hard-on. Everybody tracking? Gimme a north-south now."

The recruits again nodded in approval.

"All righty. Now, fifth thing," Murdock said in a loud voice. "Topic is race. Bottom line is this, pukes: ain't no niggers or spics or crackers 'mongst y'all's sorry asses. We's all green here, Army green. I or the other drill sergeants better not hear any of you say words like I just did. We're all Army green and we're all on the same team. It's one team, one fight here. No individuals, no heroes. No bigots, too. If we have a faggot in our ranks, tough shit. Queers can serve in Uncle Sam's Army so long as they don't start sucking dick or bending down to offer some ass. You've heard of Don't Ask Don't Tell? Well follow it. Leave the faggots alone. They're not play dolls or punching bags. Everyone clear? Tracking on this race and fag shit? Gimme a north-south now."

The C-4-10 recruits once again nodded in approval, and then Murdock said, "Last thing pukes, before I turn it over to Drill Sergeant Collinsworth who'll take y'all down to Supply for your linen. Last thing is the only authorized eyeglasses to wear are the Army-issued glasses, otherwise known as BCGs, which stands for Birth Control Glasses. Yeah, I know they're thick-frame glasses that look like shit. Hell, that's why they're called BCGs, 'cause no sorry ass wearing them could ever get laid." Murdock suddenly paused. He had a quizzical look to him.

"Hmm? Well, lemme take that one back," he said. "Maybe in Panama. I got me some fine pussy in Panama when I was stationed there. You know you can pay some *chica* five bucks to sit on your face there? Yeah, maybe some BCG-wearing dude can get laid in Panama, but the point is it ain't 'bout looks, pukes. Your ass is here to train. BCGs are good field glasses. I myself need to wear glasses when I'm qualifying with the M16, so for you four-eyes out there, the only authorized glasses are the Army-issued BCGs. I see some of y'all are already wearing them—that's good. Every four-eye 'mongst ya should've received BCGs during inprocessing week. Everybody tracking on eye glasses? Gimme a north-south, now."

The recruits in formation nodded in approval. Boudreau, himself wearing the issued BCGs, thought: *No caffeine—no problem; I'm already off that. No porn— no problem there either. Wear BCGs—I can handle that too.*

"Oh, and one very last thing, pukes—I almost forgot," said Murdock. He was still standing in front of Second Platoon, his thick Popeye forearms crossed over his chest.

"Y'all need to remember what G.I. stands for. Stands for Government Issue. That's what you pukes are—you're government issue; you're government property. And you need to take care of yourself, take care of that government property. Number one—take care of your feet. We high-speed drill sergeants will give you tips on how to avoid blisters and shit. Number two—watch the sun, especially for you white-as-a-fish-belly types like me. Use sunscreen. Your ass gets a sunburn, that's destruction of government property. That's a No Go. Bottom line pukes, you're not on the block anymore. It's the Army way now. Follow the rules, drink the fuckin' Kool Aid, and y'all be okay. Basic Training is one big Gut Check. Find it within your sorry asses to follow our orders and do what we tell y'all to do. Now lemme turn it over to Drill Sergeant Collinsworth."

CHAPTER NINE

After Murdock's rundown of the dos and don'ts of Basic Training, the C-4-10 recruits spent the remainder of the day cleaning and setting up their barracks building, which meant they mopped floors, set up bunk beds, and filled up wall lockers with military-issued clothing. It was also on Day One of Basic that Specialist Boudreau discovered his assigned Basic Training battle buddy was Private First Class James Bodette, a tall broad-shouldered fellow from the suburbs of Atlanta. Boudreau, who stood five feet-seven inches in height and weighed in at 165 pounds, gladly offered the six-foot-two, two-hundred-pound Bodette the easier-to-get-to bottom bunk. Lights Out was at 2200.

* * *

Day Two of Basic began at 0430 and started with the yell of "Wake up! Wake up you sorry asses." Then someone turned on the lights in the bay room.

Boudreau recognized the yelling as Drill Sergeant Collinsworth's voice. The bright florescent lights made his eyes squint first thing in the morning.

"Wake up Charlie-4-10 recruits. Time is 0430," yelled Collinsworth. Boudreau slowly rubbed his squinting eyes. From his top bunk he noticed Collinsworth walking the hallway.

"You all have thirty mikes to do some personal hygiene, get into your BDUs, and get in formation in the parking lot in front of the barracks," yelled Collinsworth. "Every one of you sorry asses will shave—every single morning. No exceptions. I don't give a fine fuck if your face is as smooth as a baby's ass, and you don't have a single whisker. You recruits will shave every morning. We drill sergeants will inspect your ugly faces too, so don't try to get clever with us."

Boudreau again rubbed his eyes. He quietly asked, "Sleep well, Jim?"

"Like a rock," replied Bodette who was just getting out of bed. "My arms and chest are tight as fuck from yesterday's push-ups, but I sure slept well. How 'bout you?"

"Pretty good," said Boudreau. "It's not Holiday Inn, but this ain't Burger King, right?"

Bodette smiled. "Roger that, battle buddy."

Boudreau, like the other C-4-10 recruits, brushed his teeth, shaved, quickly polished his boots, and got into his BDUs. It then took him less than five minutes to make his bunk to standards.

0445. I got plenty of time, thought Boudreau as he put the finishing touches to his bunk. *Jim's almost done with his bunk, too. Well, I guess I'll head outside and form up early.*

Boudreau headed out of the bay room, took a right, and started walking down the beige-colored tile hallway. Other recruits were in the hallway too, and his battle buddy was just some eight paces behind him. Still walking, Boudreau noticed three recruits reading a flyer thumb-tacked to a large cork board hanging on one of the hallway cinderblock walls. He stopped walking, peeked over a recruit's shoulders, and glanced at the flyer. He then turned and faced Bodette who was now just a few paces behind him.

"Hey Jim, read this," he told his battle buddy. "It's called a Hurt Feelings Report." Bodette, now standing directly behind Boudreau, peered at the flyer. The pair read the flyer along with the other three recruits:

Paul Bouchard

HURT FEELINGS REPORT *(Courtesy of Drill Sergeant Murdock)*
    Date/Time Group of Hurtfulness: _____

_____

    Name of Whiner Filing Report: _____

_____

    1. Which ear were the words of hurtfulness spoken into: Left/Right/Both? _____
    2. Is there permanent feelings damage? YES/NO _____
    3. Did you need tissue for your tears? YES/NO _____
    4. Reasons for filing report:
        I am thin skinned   YES
        I am a wuss   YES
        I am a sissy   YES
        I was beat up as a kid   YES
        I want my mommy   YES
        I cry like a little girl   YES
        All of the above   YES
    5. Name of real soldier who hurt your sensitive feelings:
_____
    6. Plan of action for whiner:
        a. If you feel you need someone to hug, go home to mommy and let her hug you and change your diaper.
        b. In case of severe hurt feelings call 1-800-CRY-BABY.

P.S. Sympathy is found between shit and syphilis in Webster's Dictionary

Boudreau smiled and exited the barracks with Bodette.

CHAPTER TEN

Boros's plan for growing, selling, and distributing marijuana in Kansas City and its environs was coming along as planned. MP Jackson was on board. Boros had promised Jackson a hundred dollars cash per week for starts, more once the drug business really got going. And as a following act, Boros had his eyes on two other potential recruits for his criminal enterprise. He was fairly certain these two recruits would also elect to join him and Jackson.

The two possible recruits came in the form of Pfc. Rivera and Pfc. Gonzalez—two buddies from San Antonio who had not only joined the Army together but had both ended up as Army mechanics stationed at Fort Leavenworth. Through some noseying around, Boros learned the tightly-knit buddies often frequented Chicas' Club—a popular Kansas City hangout—on Saturday nights.

Sipping on a Corona on one such Saturday night, Boros, an above-average charmer and salesman, introduced himself to Rivera and Gonzalez, and, as the rounds of beer kept coming, Boros kept putting on the charm, listening attentively to the conversational topics and showing an interest in all that was talked about. When he felt the situation and moment was right, Boros asked matter-of-factly, "How would you both like to make some good side money?"

CHAPTER ELEVEN

"**M**orning pukes," said the drill sergeant at the head of the C-4-10 formation.

"Morning drill sergeant," replied the C-4-10 recruits in unison.

Boudreau, part of Second Squad, First Platoon, was standing next to Bodette. He caught a glimpse of the drill sergeant's name tag, which read Carter.

Charles Carter was a six-foot-four, slim, muscular black man, who looked like a shorter version of the great San Antonio Spurs' center, David Robinson. In fact, in an earlier life, that's exactly what Carter had hoped to be—a professional basketball player. He had been a high-school and junior-college hoops star, but when he transferred into Division I at Oklahoma, Carter quickly discovered he was just an average college player. Still, he was invited to CBA tryouts after graduation, and he played two years in the CBA and one year of professional ball in Europe. But the best he could do on the basketball court was as a substitute player, a bench warmer averaging only six minutes of playing time per game. Realizing that the real professional league—the NBA—wasn't calling, Carter, at the age of twenty-six, traded in his sneakers for Army boots, and after six years in the Army, in order to further his military career, Carter became a drill sergeant.

"Game plan for today is the following," yelled Carter to the C-4-10 recruits. Boudreau couldn't help but notice how pristine and shiny Carter's boots were.

"Breakfast chow will kick off in about thirty mikes. We'll then form up outside the mess hall and march over to the Shopette to get you all some haircuts. The rest of the day will be spent practicing drill and ceremony maneuvers. Everybody tracking?"

"Hooah!" replied the recruits.

"Good," said Carter.

He then added, "If you don't have money for a haircut, then find some. Borrow from your battle buddy or borrow from some other recruit who has the dough. Haircuts are four dollars and twenty-five cents. Five bucks leaves the barber a decent seventy-five cent tip. Most of you should have that kind of money on you. If not, borrow from a battle buddy. Otherwise, there's an ATM machine at the Shopette. Remember C-4-10: one team, one fight. Everyone tracking?"

Another loud "Hooah!" from the formation of recruits.

"Good," Carter said. "Company—attention! Right face! Fall in on the lead platoon."

Two other drill sergeants chimed in with the order, "Forward."

Carter then yelled, "March!"

* * *

C-4-10 was formed up outside the red-brick mess hall at 0630. All the recruits had just eaten breakfast.

Boudreau, standing in formation, noticed the rising morning sun making itself more visible with each passing second. He guessed the temperature to be in the mid-fifties. A slight breeze was present.

"Company—Attention!" yelled the drill sergeant at the head of the C-4-10 formation. Boudreau couldn't quite make out the nametag of the slim, middle-aged drill sergeant about forty feet from him.

"At ease. Morning, C-4-10," said the drill sergeant. He surprisingly had a powerful voice for a small man.

"Morning, drill sergeant," replied the formed-up recruits.

"My name's Drill Sergeant Moran. I'll be marching you all to the Shopette this morning so you can get haircuts. After that, I'll be your drill and ceremony instructor for the day. Everyone tracking?"

"Hooah," replied the recruits.

"Excellent, excellent," said Moran in an approving tone. "Always good to stay motivated C-4-10. You all keep your heads in the game. See a fellow recruit slack off —tell his ass to shape up. Now, coupla admin issues. First, tomorrow we'll start doing our PT, our physical training. PT will be everyday 'cept for Sundays—the Lord's Day—and a few other days like when we're out in the field, although we'll do field PT when we're out in the field. Second, starting pretty soon—in a day or two—you lucky sons of bitches will get phone privileges. That means you all can use the pay phones outside the barracks, but only—and I mean only—when we release you for the day. That should be around 1900 hours."

Moran paused to gather his thoughts, then he continued.

"Now on this phone privilege stuff, let me remind you all that a privilege is just that—a privilege. It's not a right. Any of you screw up here, then we high-speed drill sergeants can revoke those phone privileges. Are we tracking Charlie-4-10?

"Hooah," replied the recruits.

"And be fair and considerate of others, pukes. A phone call shouldn't last more than ten mikes. Ten minutes maximum, gang. Your battle buddies also need to make calls. Everyone tracking?"

"Hooah," replied the C-4-10 recruits.

"Good. Third thing," said Moran, "is we'll also have Mail Call starting in a coupla days. Mail Call usually kicks off around 2000 hours and lasts for twenty mikes." He paused for just a second or two, then he said, "When you hear the music of Reveille play at 0600, you stop what you're doing, get to the position of attention, and render the proper salute. Same thing goes for Retreat, which plays at 1700. Are we tracking, Charlie-4-10?"

"Hooah," replied the recruits.

"Good," said Moran. "Now I know you all have been working on a company motto the last coupla days even when your sorry asses were back at the inprocessing phase. Let's say the company motto twice a day—first thing in the morning and right after dinner chow. That's the game plan. Are we tracking?"

"Hooah," replied the recruits.

"Excellent," said Moran, then he yelled, "Company—attention! Right-face! Forward—march!"

The recruits did the maneuvers and started marching forward in step. Moran soon broke out into a marching cadence.

Moran: "They say that in the Army, the chow is mighty fine."

C-4-10: "They say that in the Army, the chow is mighty fine."

Moran: "A chicken jumped off the table and started marking time."

C-4-10: "A chicken jumped off the table and started marking time."

Moran: "Oh, Lord I wanna go-oh."

C-4-10:" Oh, Lord I wanna go-oh."

Moran: "But they won't let me go-oh."

C-4-10: "But they won't let me go-oh. Oh, oh-oh, oh-oh-oh-oh-oh, heh!"

Moran: "They say that in the Army, the coffee's mighty fine."

C-4-10: "They say that in the Army, the coffee's mighty fine."

Moran: "It looks like muddy water and tastes like turpentine."

C-4-10: "It looks like muddy water and tastes like turpentine."

Moran: "Oh, Lord I wanna go-oh."

C-4-10: "Oh, Lord I wanna go-oh."

Moran: "But they won't let me go-oh."

C-4-10: "But they won't let me go-oh. Oh, oh-oh, oh-oh-oh-oh-oh-oh, heh!"

Moran guided the three-platoon company formation to the left by ordering "Column left—march." He then resumed his cadence.

Moran: "They say that in the Army, the pay is mighty fine."

C-4-10: "They say that in the Army, the pay is mighty fine."

Moran: "They give you a hundred dollars and take back ninety-nine."

C-4-10: "They give you a hundred dollars and take back ninety-nine."

Moran: "Oh, Lord I wanna go-oh."

C-4-10: "Oh, Lord I wanna go-oh."

Moran: "But they won't let me go-oh."

C-4-10: "But they won't let me go-oh. Oh, oh-oh, oh-oh-oh-oh-oh-oh, heh!"

Moran: "Column right—march."

The C-4-10 recruits executed a column right and then kept marching forward.

Moran: "They say that in the Army, the girls are mighty fine."

C-4-10: "They say that in the Army, the girls are mighty fine."

Moran: "They look like Phyllis Diller and march like Frankenstein."

C-4-10: "They look like Phyllis Diller and march like Frankenstein."

Moran: "Oh, Lord I wanna go-oh."

C-4-10: "Oh, Lord I wanna go-oh."

Moran: "But they won't let me go-oh."

C-4-10: "But they won't let me go-oh. Oh, oh-oh, oh-oh-oh-oh-oh-oh, heh!"

Moran kept marching the company to the Shopette while singing cadence. At one point, he again gave the command of "column left—march" to direct C-4-10 to the narrow asphalt road heading toward the Shopette. Once on the road he broke out into another cadence.

Moran: "I joined the Ar-Ar-my."
C-4-10: "I joined the Ar-Ar-my."
Moran: "So I could feel real good."
C-4-10: "So I could feel real good."
Moran: "I joined the Ar-Ar-my."
C-4-10: "I joined the Ar-Ar-my."
Moran: "So I could feel like I should."
C-4-10: "So I could feel like I should."
Moran: "Feeling good."
C-4-10: "Feeling good."
Moran: "Like I should."
C-4-10: "Like I should."
Moran: "Outta be."
C-4-10: "Outta be."
Moran: "In Hollywood."
C-4-10: "In Hollywood."
Moran: "I joined the Ar-Ar-my."
C-4-10: "I joined the Ar-Ar-my."
Moran: "I joined the Ar-Ar-my."
C-4-10: "I joined the Ar-Ar-my."
Moran: "So I could go to school."
C-4-10: "So I could go to school."
Moran: "I joined the Ar-Ar-my."
C-4-10: "I joined the Ar-Ar-my."
Moran: "So I could be real cool."
C-4-10: "So I could be real cool."
Moran: "Go to school."
C-4-10: "Go to school."
Moran: "Being cool."
C-4-10: "Being cool."
Moran: "Feeling good."
C-4-10: "Feeling good."
Moran: "Like I should."
C-4-10: "Like I should."

Moran: "Outta be."
C-4-10: "Outta be."
Moran: "In Hollywood."
C-4-10: "In Hollywood."
Moran: "I joined the Ar-Ar-my."
C-4-10: "I joined the Ar-Ar-my."
Moran: "I joined the Ar-Ar-my."
C-4-10: "I joined the Ar-Ar-my."
Moran: "So I could kill a Commy."
C-4-10: "So I could kill a Commy."
Moran: "I joined the Ar-Ar-my."
C-4-10: "I joined the Ar-Ar-my."
Moran: "So I could make Mommy happy."
C-4-10: "So I could make Mommy happy."
Moran: "Kill a Commy."
C-4-10: "Kill a Commy."
Moran: "Mommy's happy."
C-4-10: "Mommy's happy."
Moran: "Back to school."
C-4-10: "Back to school."
Moran: "Being cool."
C-4-10: "Being cool."
Moran: "Feeling good."
C-4-10: "Feeling good."
Moran: "Like I should."
C-4-10: "Like I should."
Meador: "Outta be."
C-4-10: "Outta be."
Moran: "In Hollywood."
C-4-10: "In Hollywood."
Moran: "I joined the Ar-Ar-my."
C-4-10: "I joined the Ar-Ar-my."
Moran: "I joined the Ar-Ar-my."
C-4-10: "I joined the Ar-Ar-my."
Moran: "So I could save South Korea."
C-4-10: "So I could save South Korea."
Moran: "I joined the Ar-Ar-my."

C-4-10: "I joined the Ar-Ar-my."
Moran: "So I could kill North Korea."
C-4-10: "So I could kill North Korea."
Moran: "South Korea."
C-4-10: "South Korea."
Moran: "North Korea."
C-4-10: "North Korea."
Moran: "Kill a Commy."
C-4-10: "Kill a Commy."
Moran: "Mommy's happy."
C-410: "Mommy's happy."
Moran: "Back to school."
C-4-10: "Back to school."
Moran: "Being cool."
C-4-10: "Being cool."
Moran: "Feeling good."
C-4-10: "Feeling good."
Moran: "Like I should."
C-4-10: "Like I should."
Moran: "Outta be."
C-4-10: "Outta be."
Moran: "In Hollywood."
C-4-10: "In Hollywood."
Moran: "I joined the Ar-Ar-my."
C-4-10: "I joined the Ar-Ar-my."

"Mark time—march," ordered Moran in a loud and commanding voice.

All three platoons of C-4-10 were now marching in place in a large parking lot directly in front of the Shopette that housed the barber shop.

"Company—halt. Okay Charlie-4-10, single file now, single file," ordered Moran.

"Go in the barber shop five at a time, starting from the column on the right. File from the right, column right!"

The first recruit in the far right column correctly yelled "Column right!" while the other lead recruits of the other columns yelled "Stand fast!"

Moran then yelled, "March," and that's when the first five recruits of the far-right column executed a column-right and entered the barber shop. Boudreau, a Second Squad member, meaning he was in the second column, stood directly ahead of his battle buddy, Bodette.

"At ease, Charlie-4-10," ordered Moran. "And no talking, privates, no talking in formation. After you get your haircuts you can walk back to the barracks and tidy up your lockers and bunks some more. Formation will be at 1000 hours outside the barracks. As for now, you shit-for-brains can pull out your SMART books and start learning shit."

Every recruit reached into one of his BDU pant cargo pockets and pulled out his SMART book, a small but thick how-to book issued to every recruit during inprocessing week. The SMART book covered every aspect of Basic Training including how to assemble and properly fire the M16 weapon, how to properly don the gas mask, how to prevent and treat cold weather and also hot weather injuries, how to read maps, how to do first aid, what the General Orders are, what the Code of Conduct is—absolutely everything was covered in the SMART book.

Suddenly, Drill Sergeant Moran yelled, "Boudreau—who's your battle buddy?"

Boudreau, engrossed in his SMART book and its material, looked up and said, "Private First Class Bodette, drill sergeant."

"Bodette—twenty push-ups," ordered Moran in a loud, powerful voice.

Damn it—what the hell did I do wrong? Boudreau wondered. *I must have fucked up somehow because my battle buddy's doing push-ups.* He was tense, nervous, also embarrassed.

What the hell did I do wrong? What's my screw up?

"One, drill sergeant, two, drill sergeant, three, drill sergeant," said Bodette who was directly behind Boudreau. He was knocking out the push-ups.

Damn it—what was my screw up? Boudreau kept thinking. He looked down at the asphalt, ashamed. Suddenly it hit him— he saw something while looking down at the pavement.

Shit. I didn't button up my cargo pocket after I pulled out my SMART book. His cargo pocket hugging his right thigh was still open. *Crap— unbuttoned buttons are a No Go. Now Jim's paying for my mistake.*

He quickly buttoned up the cargo pocket.

"Eighteen, drill sergeant, nineteen, drill sergeant, twenty, drill sergeant," said Bodette, his voice struggling as he knocked out the last push-ups.

He struggled to say, "Drill sergeant—permission to recover?" as he remained in the front-lean-and-rest position, the standard push-up position.

"Recover Private Bodette," Moran said. "That'll teach Boudreau not to leave his BDU buttons open."

CHAPTER TWELVE

The product of a broken, white, working-class home, Dustin Boros, now twenty two, grew up in a poor, mostly black section of Newark, New Jersey. His father, David Boros, was a house-painter and part-time cab driver. His mother—long out of the picture—suffered from bipolar, manic-depressive disorder and lived somewhere in South Florida with friends. Dustin's sister, Nicole, two years his junior, was last heard from in Phoenix, Arizona, where she apparently was running with some motorcycle gang.

Like many of the kids he grew up with, Dustin Boros had some brushes with the law. At fifteen, came a shoplifting charge; at sixteen, it was a drug possession. There was also a trespassing violation at age seventeen, but that was later dropped on account of a legal technicality. Bored, restless, and hating minimum wage jobs—which were all he could find with his GED—Boros decided to switch gears and enlist in the military.

Of course, the whole military enlistment thing wasn't easy—not with his legal infractions—which was why the Air Force, Navy, and Marines all rejected him. But then came luck, the type of luck brought about when preparation meets opportunity. The preparation came in the form of a thirsty Boros desperate for a change, while opportunity came in the form of a middle-aged, crafty, and crooked Army recruiter named Mike Michelsen. Michelsen was adept at pushing through fraudulent enlistment papers, and when the young, thirsty, nineteen-year-old Boros came by his recruiting station, Michelsen put his skills to work. That's how Boros was able to join the Army—his recruiter simply left all the criminal stuff off the paperwork.

Boros reported to Fort Jackson, South Carolina, in the spring of 1991, the site of his Basic Training. That training went well but uneventfully. Boros didn't stand out or win awards; he simply followed orders, met the training standards, and surprisingly kept out of trouble. Upon completing his AIT training at Fort Lee, Virginia, the newly minted Army supply clerk received orders to the famed 101st Airborne Division based at Fort Campbell, Kentucky, and it was while stationed at Campbell that the young, ambitious, and money-hungry Boros discovered just how profitable the marijuana trade could be.

Money, man—there's a shit load of money with pot, Boros thought as he was driving back from Clarksville, Tennessee, after a small drop-off for a drug dealer.

Fuck man, I remember selling crack in Newark, but there was puny money in that for us street peddlers. Money's always at the top. It's the Big Dawgs who make the good money. And there's plenty of money with the Mary Jane stuff. I need to learn me this business. I'll be the good little street peddler again for some time, learn the business and shit, but eventually, I'll run my own show. Big bucks, man. Big bucks brings the chicks, the nice clothes, the nice wheels, the nice sound systems in those nice wheels. Yessir, I'll be running my own show some day.

CHAPTER THIRTEEN

Ten minutes after the unbuttoned cargo-pocket fiasco, Boudreau found himself sitting in one of the five barber chairs. He saw Bodette occupy the chair to his left.

"Sorry 'bout those push-ups, battle buddy."

"No worries," replied Bodette. "I need to work on my push-ups anyway."

Still feeling bad, Boudreau said, "Do your boots and bunk as a sign of goodwill?"

"Deal," said Bodette, smiling.

Standing behind Boudreau was a tall, slim barber, sporting a thin white overcoat. By looking at the large mirror in front of him, Boudreau could see the barber behind him. Boudreau guessed the barber was in his early sixties. He noticed the barber had thick eye glasses, resembling Army issue birth-control glasses. He also noticed the barber had thick, bushy eyebrows.

"You'll get several of these haircuts while in Basic, son," said the barber as he began shearing Boudreau's head with a hair clipper. "Ain't nothing to it really."

Not sure what to say, Boudreau simply replied, "Yes, sir."

"Army's sure changed since I was in, son. I'm a Korean and Vietnam War veteran, you know."

"Thank you for your service," replied Boudreau as the barber kept clipping his hair and vigorously maneuvering the hair clipper.

"Well, thank you, son. Yep, I got me a Bronze Star and two Purple Hearts, too. 'Been there and done that' as the young'uns say." He stepped to Boudreau's left and started shearing the left side of Boudreau's scalp.

"Yep, Army's lot different now—lots easier. Less discipline if you ask me, and that's Clinton's fault right there is what that is. Clinton was raised Baptist, but he ain't no Baptist by my book, and my book's the Bible. Read the Bible any, son?"

"Yessir," replied Boudreau, but only to appease the barber. The fact was, Boudreau, though Catholic and an occasional Mass goer, didn't read the Bible.

"Yep, Clinton's letting fags in the military now. Wasn't like that back in my day, son. If there were fags back then they were the closest types, I promise you that."

Boudreau said nothing.

The barber did a few final touches to Boudreau's scalp, then he spun Boudreau around so Boudreau faced the mirror. The barber unsnapped and removed Boudreau's protective apron.

"There you go, son," said the barber in a hurried tone. Boudreau, now directly facing the large mirror, saw that he was completely bald. He reached into his back right pocket, pulled out his wallet, and removed a five-dollar bill.

"Appreciate that, son," the barber said as Boudreau handed him the money. "And you keep readin' that Bible now, you hear."

CHAPTER FOURTEEN

P ernell Jackson grew up in a tough, crime-infested section
of Gary, Indiana. He was the oldest of four children, all of
whom were raised by their mom, Yvonne, because their dad—
Yvonne never revealed his name to the kids—had long been
gone and had never done anything in the way of love, caring,
and financial support.

Pernell was a decent kid up to the age of twelve. That's when
he started hanging with the wrong crowd and started doing the
wrong things like petty theft and selling drugs. And like the
members of that wrong crowd, Pernell quit high school as soon
as he was able to, and also like them, he kept selling drugs. He
also took on minimum-wage jobs to help make ends meet.

The life of drug selling coupled with minimum-wage jobs
lasted two years for Pernell, and it came to an end with a chance
meeting with one of his step uncles, Al Carter, a retired Army
first sergeant, who told his nephew about the Army and its
benefits such as a steady paycheck, the chance to see the world,
and free health care.

"You might even be able to sign up Yvonne, your dear
mother, as a dependent and get her better health care," Carter
told his nephew during the chance meeting. "Think 'bout it,
Pernell— it's a step up."

And Jackson did think about it; he wrestled with the thought
of how to improve his lot in life—how to take a "step up," how
to stop spinning his wheels, and how to start getting some

real traction so he could move forward and better himself. And the more he thought about it, the more enlisting in the Army made sense. And so he did; he enlisted in the Army. He was all of nineteen at the time. His Basic Training took place at Fort Jackson, South Carolina, and like some other Basic Training recruits, Jackson had no idea what his MOS (military occupational specialty or job) would be until week three of Basic.

That's when he heard from one of the drill sergeants, "Congrats, Private Jackson. You've been selected for MP training after Basic," to which the novice Jackson's immediate response was:

"What's MP training?"

"Military Police, son," responded the drill sergeant. "It's a good career field. Civilian police departments are constantly hiring, so you'll have great job prospects in civilian life if you decide to get out of the Army once your enlistment term ends."

Man, imagine that, thought Jackson as soon as he heard the term "military police." *A policeman, a cop. Brothers back home sure will get a kick outta this: Pernell Jackson—gone to the dark side, gone blue, became a cop. Shiiiiiit.*

After his military training, Jackson reported to his first duty station, Fort Leavenworth, Kansas, and it was there that he met the ambitious and charismatic Boros, who recruited him to sell and transport drugs.

Some say there's nothing worse than a crooked cop. Pernell Jackson, now twenty two, was the Army equivalent of a crooked cop—he was a crooked MP who wanted to make more money, and that's precisely what Boros had in mind. He wanted a cop to be part of his outfit; he wanted someone on the inside if things were to get messy.

CHAPTER FIFTEEN

Charlie-4-10 was awarded phone privileges starting on the second day of Basic. That evening—the second day of Basic Training—Boudreau polished his boots and prepared his BDUs for the next day's training, and once done with those chores, he, like most of the recruits, got in line behind one of the five phone booths adjacent to the barracks. He got on a phone at 9:15 and immediately called Cindy.

Two rings—no answer.

Four rings—still no answer.

After six rings, the answering machine picked up, and Boudreau heard "Hi. You've reached Cindy and Jack. We're not in right now, so please leave a message."

Hmmn, that's weird, he thought as he stood in the tight-fitting phone booth. *Cindy should be home.*

The answering machine's beep sound suddenly kicked in.

"Uh, Cindy, it's me, Jack. We've got phone privileges here in Basic. All's well. Miss you lots. Hugs and kisses from me. Send my best to the gang. I love you. I'll call again this week." Then he hung up the phone.

CHAPTER SIXTEEN

"**F**ormation outside at 0500, pukes," yelled Drill Sergeant Murdock. He was walking through the barrack's hallway as recruits were hurriedly getting out of bed.

"Uniform for this morning will be the PT uniform. Oh five hundred, pukes. This will be your first PT session. Get used to it because we're gonna do lots of PT here. Oh, and everyone bring a full canteen of water too."

The entire C-4-10 company was formed up by 0500 outside the barracks. Every recruit was wearing his PT uniform: Army gray PT tee-shirt, Army gray PT shorts, white socks, running shoes, and a yellow reflector belt around his waist. Every recruit also hand-held a green plastic canteen full of water. Murdock, standing at the head of the company formation, was dressed in his BDUs. Boudreau, standing in Second Squad of First Platoon, noticed that drill sergeants Carter, Moran, and Collinsworth were wearing their PT uniforms.

"How about you shit-for-brain pukes sound off with your company motto?" Murdock said. "And be sure to sound off like you gotta a pair. Everybody tracking?"

"Hooah," replied the recruits who were still standing at the position of parade rest.

Murdock yelled, "Company—attention!" and the C-4-10 recruits immediately assumed the position of attention and sounded off with their company song:

The Law.

This is the House of Pain.

Are we not men? No, we are not men. We are beasts.

And Charlie Company has made us beasts.

We will not walk, we will not talk, we will not gather in the night.

We are highly trained to kill.

Our last resort is cold steel.

Jab, between the second and third rib.

Twist.

Aaaaaaah—hooah!

"Excellent. Excellent, Charlie-4-10," said Murdock with a smile. He quickly turned his head down and to the left and spat some tobacco juice on the ground. "At ease. Not bad, pukes. Gotta give y'all a north-south for that one." He immediately nodded in approval and then said, "All righty, C-4-10. Game plan for this morning is PT. Physical training is part of the Army lifestyle so y'all better get with the program and drink the Kool Aid. Some of you sorry pukes are in decent shape, and some y'all ain't. Every single one of y'all has to pass a PT test to graduate from Basic. We will do PT six days a week. Day off is the Lord's Day. That's when most of you sorry asses will go to church and thank God you still have a pair. It's also the day when y'all will do clean-up details and read your SMART books."

Murdock again spat some tobacco juice on the ground.

"Drill Sergeants Carter, Collinsworth, and Moran will do PT with you pukes this morning. Remember pukes—y'all are GIs. Y'all are Government Issue and Government Property. Take care of that property; take care of your bodies. I want every single Charlie-4-10 recruit to pass the final PT Test. I don't give a crap if you were some candy-ass, couch-potato, civilian puke back in civilian life. Y'all will PT here and get in shape. Tracking C-4-10?"

"Hooah," replied the recruits.

"Good. Coupla more admin things before I turn it over to high-speed, low-drag Drill Sergeant Carter. Starting this evening, the upcoming week's training events will be posted on the hallway board next to the HURT FEELINGS REPORT. By the way, have y'all seen and read that high-speed report? Yes? No?" Murdock, smiling, quickly scanned the company formation. "Everybody tracking 'bout that report?'

"Hooah," replied the C-4-10 recruits.

"Excellent, excellent. Hey y'all, if anyone of you sorry asses gets his feelings hurt here and wants to go back home to Fort Living Room and to Mommy, then just fill out that form. You wanna return to being a civilian puke, to go back to your job at McDonalds or Taco Bell—or some shit like that—just fill out that form. Are we tracking Charlie-4-10?"

Another loud "hooah" from the formation of recruits.

"Good. Now, like I was saying, we'll be posting the week's training plan on the hallway board. Look at that plan every night before you give your eyelids a rest and get some shuteye. As you train here during Basic, y'all also have some details to do like grass cutting details over at battalion, KP duty—that stands for Kitchen Police where y'all help clean the mess hall tables and take out the garbage—and then there's CQ duty. That stands for Charge of Quarters. That's you being on a thirty-minute night-watch shift to make sure the barracks are safe, doors are locked, and all your battle buddies are catching some zzzzs. Y'all have CQ duty 'bout every third night or so. Uniform for all the details is the BDU except for CQ which is your PT uniform and a flashlight. Tracking Charlie-4-10?"

"Hooah," replied the recruits.

"All righty, then," said Murdock. He again quickly spat tobacco juice on the ground. "Just keep an eye on the details roster, and y'all have yourselves a fine Army Day." He then turned toward Drill Sergeant Carter.

"Drill Sergeant Carter—company's yours. These pukes need some PT."

Drill Sergeant Carter briskly walked to the head of the formation. He faced the recruits and ordered, "Company—attention. Right—face. Forward—march," and in less than fifteen minutes the C-4-10 recruits found themselves in the middle of a quarter-mile runner's track that was oval-shaped with a four-lane running surface made of a red cushiony and rubbery material. Thin white lines demarcated the running lanes of the track.

Carter formed up the company in the center grass area of the track. Boudreau, a bit chilly and firmly holding on to his plastic green canteen in his right hand, noticed four bright spotlights atop four telephone poles illuminating the entire track area. With the exception of the brightly lit track, the surrounding areas were nothing more than pitch-black darkness.

Drill Sergeant Collinsworth walked over to Drill Sergeant Carter and handed him a black bullhorn.

"Good morning Charlie-4-10!" yelled Carter into the bullhorn. His voice now had a tinge of a mechanical sound to it. "Your first PT session—let's have ourselves a fine Army morning. Can I get a big C-4-10 hooah on that?"

"Hooah!" yelled the recruits.

"Okay Charlie-4-10, here we go!" yelled the tall and muscular Carter from the head of the formation. He then gave the following commands:

"Extend to the left—march. Arms downward—move. Left-face. Extend to the left—march. Arms downward—move. Right-face. From front-to-rear, count-off."

Each row of recruits, representing the four squads of each platoon—sounded off with their respective "One," "Two," "Three," "Four."

Carter then said, "Even numbers to the left—uncover. At-ease."

There was a brief pause, then Carter said, "All right Charlie-4-10, let's kick off this PT session by doing some stretching exercises."

Carter led the recruits through various rotational exercises: the neck rotation, the arm-and-shoulder rotation, the hip rotation, and the knees-and-ankle rotation. That was followed by some stretching exercises including the overhead arm pull, the abdominal stretch, the chest stretch, the hamstring stretch, and the standing groin stretch. Altogether, the rotational and stretching exercises took ten minutes to complete.

"Okay privates, I'm gonna take it easy on you this morning as far as push-ups and sit-ups go," Carter said. He was still using the bullhorn. "That's because A, I'm a nice guy, and B, I know you sorry asses are still sore from the push-ups y'all did when you first got off those cattle trucks." Carter paused for just a second, then he said, "This morning's PT session will focus on grass drills and running. We's still gonna do push-ups and sit-ups, though, but just a few of them."

Carter led the C-4-10 recruits through three sets of twenty-count sit-ups, with one set being Rocky-style sit-ups followed by a set of regular sit-ups, then topped off by a set of crunches-style sit-ups. After the set of crunches Carter ordered the one hundred and twenty or so recruits to lay flat on the ground, their stomachs flat on the grass.

"Okay privates, grass-drill time," said Carter, still using the bullhorn to amplify his voice. "Rollover privates, rollover—roll like a log. Now get on your backs. Backs on the ground, y'all. Good, now we's gonna do some flutter-kicks. The flutter-kick is a four-count exercise, privates. In cadence—exercise!"

Carter: "One-two-three."

C-4-10: "One."

Carter: "One-two-three."

C-4-10: "Two."

Carter: "One-two-three."

C-4-10: "Three."

Carter: "One-two-three."

C-4-10: "Four."

It went on like this until the C-4-10 recruits reached the count of thirty. Boudreau, with his stomach and leg muscles tightening up, was still a bit chilly but the exercises were quickly warming him up.

"Now on your bellies, privates," ordered Carter. "Bellies on the ground. Hurry—move!"

The C-4-10 recruits did as ordered. Their stomachs were on the cold dew-filled grass.

"Now roll, privates—roll your entire bodies to the right!" yelled Carter. "Roll like a log y'all."

The recruits did as ordered and rolled their bodies to the right.

"Now to the left, privates," ordered Carter as he started walking around the PT formation.

"Roll to the left now."

The C-4-10 recruits did as ordered. Boudreau, still in the second row of First Platoon, felt his head getting a bit dizzy from changing direction.

"Okay, good privates—good job!" yelled Carter into the bullhorn. He started pacing around the recruits.

"Feel that pain, y'all? Feel your stomach and legs burning? Good. Remember what Drill Sergeant Murdock said when you pukes got off that cattle truck. He said 'pain is good; pain is just weakness leaving the body.' I see lots of y'all in pain. Y'all weak, man, but we'll make soldiers outta y'all's sorry asses."

Carter then started pacing around the PT formation, the bullhorn firmly in his right hand. Some faint moans and groans could be heard from the recruits who were still on the ground, their bellies on the cold wet grass. Boudreau looked to his left and saw Bodette wincing in pain, his face contorted, his eyes squinting and almost shut.

"Anyone of you pukes know what makes the green grass grow?" asked Carter as he paced around the recruits. "Anyone? What makes the green grass grow y'all?"

None of the recruits spoke.

"Bright, red blood, privates. Red blood is what makes the green grass grow," said Carter. "Are we tracking?"

"Hooah," replied the C-4-10 recruits as they lay on the ground. Boudreau, feeling cold in the hip region, looked at his shorts.

Man, my shorts are dark gray and cold from absorbing all that dew on the grass.

"That's right," said Carter. "Heh, y'all, it's just like the movie *Patton* where George C. Scott stands in front of Old Glory. Remember what Patton said, privates. He said, 'The object of war is not to die for your country. The object of war is to have the other sumbitch die for his.' Are we tracking, Charlie-4-10?"

"Hooah," replied the recruits.

"Remember that, y'all. You want that red blood on the grass to be enemy red blood. Make the green grass grow with enemy blood. We all tracking Charlie-4-10?"

"Hooah," replied the recruits.

"Good," yelled Carter. "All right now, everybody give me ten push-ups, then y'all can stretch out on your own for 'bout two or three mikes. After that we's going on a run, Charlie-4-10—not on the runner's track surrounding y'all right now. No, we'll be running on the roads around here."

Boudreau, like the other recruits, did his ten push-ups, then he started doing some leg-stretching exercises to get ready for the run. He also did a few jumping jacks to warm himself up.

Time to do some running, he thought. *I'm cold and sore right now, but I think I'll hold my own on this run. I should, man. I'm used to jogging four-five miles a day.*

"How you holding up, Jack?"

Boudreau stopped stretching and turned to his left. It was Bodette.

"Not bad, battle buddy. How 'bout yourself?"

"Chest and stomach are tight as fuck," said an out-of-breath Bodette. "I just hope this run ain't gonna be too long."

"You'll be okay, Jim. Just—"

"Company—attention!" yelled Carter, now standing in front of the three-platoon formation. He handed the bullhorn to Drill Sergeant Collinsworth.

"At ease. Everybody drink some H-2-0; everybody drink some water from y'all's canteens. Yeah it's a bit chilly right now, but your bodies still need to hydrate. Drink water! Drink water!"

The recruits did as ordered and drank from their canteens.

* * *

A few minutes later, Carter called C-4-10 to attention and marched them to a nearby gravel road. He yelled "Double time" to which the recruits responded with "anytime," and that's when the entire company picked up a light jog and Carter broke out into a run cadence:

Carter: "One."

C-4-10: "One."

Carter: "Two."

C-4-10: "Two."

Carter: "Three."

C-4-10: "Three."

Carter: "Four."

C-4-10: "Fire up now."

Carter: "When my granny was ninety-two."

C-4-10: "When my granny was ninety-two."

Carter: "She did PT better than you."

C-4-10: "She did PT better than you."

Carter: "When my granny was ninety-three."

C-4-10: "When my granny was ninety-three."

Carter: "She did PT better than me."

C-4-10: "She did PT better than me."

Carter: "When my granny was ninety-four."

C-4-10: When my granny was ninety-four."

Carter: "She did PT more and more."

C-4-10: "She did PT more and more."

Carter: "And when my granny was ninety-five."

C-4-10: "And when my granny was ninety-five."

Carter: "She did PT to stay alive."

C-4-10: "She did PT to stay alive."

Carter: "When my granny was ninety-six."

C-4-10: "When my granny was ninety-six."

Carter: "She did PT just for kicks."

C-4-10: "She did PT just for kicks."

Carter: "And when my granny was ninety-seven."

C-4-10: "And when my granny was ninety-seven."

Carter: "She upped, she died, she went to heaven."

C-4-10: "She upped, she died, she went to heaven."

Carter: "She met Saint Peter at the Pearly Gates, and he said, 'Drop down granny and give me ten. 'Cause I'm hard core."

C-4-10: "Hard core."
Carter: "Airborne."
C-4-10: "Airborne."
Carter: "Ranger."
C-4-10: "Ranger."
Carter: "Danger."
C-4-10: "Danger."
Carter: "Locked and cocked."
C-4-10: "Locked and cocked."
Carter: "Ready to rock."
C-4-10: "Ready to rock."
Carter: "Kill a Commy."
C-4-10: "Kill a Commy."
Carter: "Mommy's happy."
C-4-10: "Mommy's happy."
Carter: "Feeling good."
C-4-10: "Feeling good."
Carter: "Like I should."
C-4-10: "Like I should."
Carter: "Outta be."
C-4-10: "Outta be."
Carter: "In Hollywood."
C-4-10: "In Hollywood."

Carter guided the running formation to another dirt road, this one stretching out through some wooded hills. Boudreau, familiar with jogging speeds, guessed the running pace to be around a ten-minute-mile clip. He noticed the first signs of a sunrise toward the east, a small orange ball creeping up between two wooded hills.

Carter: "'Cause I'm Aeh-eye."
C-4-10: "AI."
Carter: "R-bee."
C-4-10: "RB."
Carter: "Oh-R."

C-4-10: "OR."
Carter: "N-ee."
C-4-10: "NE."
Carter: "What's that spell?"
C-4-10: "Airborne."
Carter: "Whatacha got?"
C-4-10: "Airborne."
Carter: "Left, left, left-right or left."
C-4-10: "Left, left, left-right or left."
Carter: "Left, left, keep it in step."
C-4-10: "Left, left, keep it in step."
Carter: "When I say one, you say two."
C-4-10: "When he says one, we say two."
Carter: "When I say red-white, you say blue."
C-4-10: "When he says red-white, we say blue."
Carter: "One."
C-4-10: "Two."
Carter: "Red-white."
C-4-10: "Blue."
Carter: "When I say three, you say four."
C-4-10: "When he says three, we say four."
Carter: "When I say gimme, you say some more."
C-4-10: "When he says gimme, we say some more."
Carter: "One."
C-4-10: "Two."
Carter: "Red-white."
C-4-10: "Blue."
Carter: "Three."
C-4-10: "Four."
Carter: "Gimme."
C-4-10: "Some more."
Carter: "When I say five, you say six."
C-4-10: "When he says five, we say six."
Carter: "When I say PT, you say for kicks."
C-4-10: "When he says PT, we say for kicks."
Carter: "One."
C-4-10: "Two."

Carter: "Red-white."
C-4-10: "Blue."
Carter: "Three."
C-4-10: "Four."
Carter: "Gimme."
C-4-10: "Some more."
Carter: "Five."
C-4-10: "Six."
Carter: "PT."
C-4-10: "For kicks."
Carter: "When I say seven, you say eight."
C-4-10: "When he says seven, we say eight."
Carter: "When I say feeling, you say great."
C-4-10: "When he says feeling, we say great."
Carter: "One."
C-4-10: "Two."
Carter: "Red-white."
C-4-10: "Blue."
Carter: "Three."
C-4-10: "Four."
Carter: "Gimme."
C-4-10: "Some more."
Carter: "Five."
C-4-10: "Six."
Carter: "PT."
C-4-10: "For kicks."
Carter: "Seven."
C-4-10: "Eight."
Carter: "Feeling."
C-4-10: "Great."
Carter: "When I say nine, you say ten."
C-4-10: "When he says nine, we say ten."
Carter: "When I say do it, you say again."
C-4-10: "When he says do it, we say again."
Carter: "One."
C-4-10: "Two."
Carter: "Red-white."

C-4-10: "Blue."

Carter: "Three."

C-410: "Four."

Carter: "Gimme."

C-4-10: "Some more."

Carter: "Five."

C-4-10: "Six."

Carter: "PT."

C-4-10: "For kicks."

Carter: "Seven."

C-4-10: "Eight."

Carter: "Feeling."

C-4-10: "Great."

Carter: "Nine."

C-4-10: "Ten."

Carter: "Do it."

C-4-10: "Again."

Carter: "Left, left, left-right your left."

C-4-10: "Left, left, left-right your left."

Carter: "Left, left, keep it in step."

C-4-10: "Left, left, keep it in step."

Carter: "Hey ladi dadi."

C-4-10: "Heh heh."

Carter: "Hey ladi dadi dough."

C-4-10: "Heh heh."

Carter: "Hey ladi dadi."

C-4-10: "Heh heh."

Carter: "Hey ladi dadi dough."

C-4-10: "Heh heh."

Carter: "I used to date a beauty queen."

C-4-10: "Heh heh."

Carter: "Now I date my M16."

C-4-10: "Heh heh."

Carter: "I used to date a beauty queen."

C-4-10: "Heh heh."

Carter: "Now I date my M16."

C-4-10: Heh heh."

Carter: "Hey ladi dadi."
C-4-10: "Heh heh."
Carter: "Heh ladi dadi dough."
C-4-10: "Heh heh."
Carter: "Heh ladi dadi."
C-4-10: "Heh heh."
Carter: "Heh ladi dadi dough."
C-4-10: "Heh heh."
Carter: "I used to be a high-school stud."
C-4-10: "Heh heh."
Carter: "Now I'm rolling in the mud."
C-4-10: "Heh heh."
Carter: "I used to be a high-school stud."
C-4-10: "Heh heh."
Carter: "Now I'm rolling in the mud."
C-4-10: "Heh heh."
Carter: "Hey ladi dadi."
C-4-10: "Heh heh."
Carter: "Heh ladi dadi dough."
C-4-10: "Heh heh."
Carter: "Hey ladi dadi."
C-4-10: "Heh heh."
Carter: "Heh ladi dadi dough."
C-4-10: "Heh heh."

Carter guided the formation up a slight hill, then he resumed his run cadence.

Carter: "I used to wear my faded jeans."
C-4-10: "Heh heh."
Carter: "Now I'm wearing Army greens."
C-4-10: "Heh heh."
Carter: "I used to wear my faded jeans."
C-4-10: "Heh heh."
Carter: "Now I'm wearing Army greens."
C-4-10: "Heh heh."
Carter: "Hey ladi dadi."
C-4-10: "Heh heh."
Carter: "Heh ladi dadi dough."

C-4-10: "Heh heh."
Carter: "Heh ladi dadi."
C-4-10: "Heh heh."
Carter: "Heh ladi dadi dough."
C-4-10: "Heh heh."
Carter: "I used to eat at Mickey Dees."
C-4-10: "Heh heh."
Carter: "Now I'm eating MREs."
C-4-10: "Heh heh."
Carter: "I used to eat at Mickey Dees."
C-4-10: "Heh heh."
Carter: "Now I'm eating MREs."
C-4-10: "Heh heh."
Carter: "Heh ladi dadi."
C-4-10: "Heh heh."
Carter: "Heh ladi dadi dough."
C-4-10: "Heh heh."
Carter: "Heh ladi dadi."
C-4-10: "Heh heh."
Carter: "Heh ladi dadi dough."
C-4-10: "Heh heh."
Carter: "I used to drive a Cadillac."
C-4-10: "Heh heh."
Carter: "Now I hump it on my back."
C-4-10: "Heh heh."
Carter: "I used to drive a Cadillac."
C-4-10: "Heh heh."
Carter: "Now I hump it on my back."
C-4-10: "Heh heh."
Carter went right into another cadence.
Carter: "G.I. beans and G.I. gravy."
C-4-10: "G.I. beans and G.I. gravy."
Carter: "Gee, I wish I had joined the Navy."
C-4-10: "Gee, I wish I had joined the Navy."
Carter: "If the wimp can't hang."
C-4-10: "If the wimp can't hang."
Carter: "Then the wimp shouldn't of came."

C-4-10: "Then the wimp shouldn't of came."
Carter: "'Cause it's one mile."
C-4-10: "One mile."
Carter: "No sweat."
C-4-10: "No sweat."
Carter: "Two miles."
C-4-10: "Two miles."
Carter: "Better yet."
C-4-10: "Better yet."
Carter: "Three miles."
C-4-10: "Three miles."
Carter: "Tons of fun."
C-4-10: "Tons of fun."
Carter: "Four miles."
C-4-10: "Four miles."
Carter: "More fun."
C-4-10: "More fun."
Carter: "'Cause I'm motivated."
C-4-10: "Motivated."
Carter: "Dedicated."
C-4-10: "Dedicated."
Carter: "Airborne."
C-4-10: "Airborne."
Carter: "Ranger."
C-4-10: "Ranger."

Carter, leading the formation, paused for a few seconds, then he sang out, "Left, left, left- right or left."

C-4-10: "Left, left, left-right or left."
Carter: "Left, left, keep it in step."
C-4-10: "Left, left, keep it in step."
Carter: "If I die on the Russian front."
C-4-10: "If I die on the Russian front."
Carter: "Bury me with a Russian cunt."
C-4-10: "Bury me with a Russian cunt."
Carter: "And if I die in a lot of mud."
C-4-10: "And if I die in a lot of mud."
Carter: "Bury me with a case of Bud."

C-4-10: "Bury me with a case of Bud."
Carter: "And if I die on the old drop zone."
C-4-10: "And if I die on the old drop zone."
Carter: "Box me up and ship me home."
C-4-10: "Box me up and ship me home."
Carter: "Tell my Momma I did my best."
C-4-10: "Tell my Momma I did my best."
Carter: "And bury me in the lean-and-rest."
C-4-10: "And bury me in the lean-and-rest."
Carter: "'Cause I'm hard core."
C-4-10: "Hard core."
Carter: "Airborne."
C-4-10: "Airborne."
Carter: "Ranger."
C-4-10: "Ranger."
Carter: "Danger."
C-4-10: "Danger."
Carter: "Super trooper."
C-4-10: "Super trooper."
Carter paused as he thought of another cadence.

He said, "Keep up with me y'all. This ain't no fast pace now. Gotta work y'alls bodies. Too many of you pukes have been living on Twinkies back in y'all's Fort Living Room days."

Boudreau, jogging with the others and breaking out into a sweat thought, *This is a good running pace, and I know all of the cadences 'cause we learned them all back during inprocessing week.*

Carter: "Coon skin and alligator hide."
C-4-10: "Coon skin and alligator hide."
Carter: "Makes a pair of jump boots just the right size."
C-4-10: "Makes a pair of jump boots just the right size."
Carter: "Stand them up, lace them up, put them on your feet."
C-4-10: "Stand them up, lace them up, put them on your feet."
Carter: "A good pair of jump boots can't be beat."
C-4-10: "A good pair of jump boots can't be beat."

Carter then yelled out, "For this next cadence respond with 'boom boom," and then he sang out ...

Carter: "What's the sound of artillery?"

C-4-10: "Boom boom."

Carter: "Shoot, move on the enemy."

C-4-10: "Boom boom."

Carter: "What's the sound that makes the earth shake?"

C-4-10: "Boom boom."

Carter: "Shoot, move, and communicate."

On it went like this—Carter guiding the recruits in a run, singing cadence. After thirty minutes of jogging he ordered, "Quick-time—march!" and the C-4-10 recruits followed the command and immediately started walking in unison. Carter then started a marching cadence.

Carter: "My recruiter told me a lie."

C-4-10: "My recruiter told me a lie."

Carter: "He said join the Army and learn to fly."

C-4-10: "Join the Army and learn to fly."

Carter: "I signed my name on the dotted line."

C-4-10: "I signed my name on the dotted line."

Carter: "Now all I do is double-time."

C-4-10: "Now all I do is double-time."

Carter: "Oh halo, oh halo, oh halo halo infantry."

C-4-10: "Oh halo, oh halo, oh halo halo infantry."

Carter: "The infantry life's the life for me."

C-4-10: "The infantry life's the life for me."

Carter: "Oh, nothing in this world is free."

C-4-10: "Oh, nothing in this world is free."

Carter: "The infantry life's the life for me."

C-4-10: "The infantry life's the life for me."

Carter: "They sat me in a barber's chair."

C-4-10: "They sat me in a barber's chair."

Carter: "They spun me around, I had no hair."

C-4-10: "They spun me around, I had no hair."

Carter: "They sat me in a barber's chair."

C-4-10: "They sat me in a barber's chair."

Carter: "They spun me around, I had no hair."

C-4-10: "They spun me around, I had no hair."
Carter: "Oh halo, oh halo, oh halo halo infantry."
C-4-10: "Oh halo, oh halo, oh halo halo infantry."
Carter: "The infantry life's the life for me."
C-4-10: "The infantry life's the life for me."
Carter: "Oh, nothing in this world is free."
C-4-10: "Oh, nothing in this world is free."
Carter: "The infantry life's the life for me."
C-4-10: "The infantry life's the life for me."

The C-4-10 formation, still on a gravel road and still marching to the marching cadences of Drill Sergeant Carter, came upon a hill crest. Down below and slightly to the west, the PT running track was in sight, and to the east, between two wooded hills, was the full circle of an orange morning sun. Boudreau, marching in step and singing out the cadences like the other recruits, was now fully warmed up and sweating. His BCG glasses were slightly fogged up from the heat he generated. He thought, *that wasn't so bad—grass drills and a nice run. I'm gonna make it through this Basic Training thing.*

"Company—halt," Carter suddenly ordered. He was directly facing and centered on the formation.

"Left-face. At-ease. All right Charlie-4-10, that was a good run. Something a bit different today, pukes. I just got word from Drill Sergeant Moran that y'all will have the afternoon off from training today on account of President Nixon's state funeral. We lost one of our former Commanders in Chief and, in proper military fashion, we will honor his life by not training today. This means your place of duty today is the barracks. Clean up your barracks this morning, and then we'll do lunch chow. Then we will all meet in the large dayroom to watch the state funeral on TV. We will meet at 1400 hours, and every one of y'all will attentively watch President Nixon's state funeral. U.S. flags will be at half mast today, and your uniform for the day is the BDU. Everyone tracking?"

"Hooah," replied the recruits in unison.

"Good," said Carter. "Again, good run Charlie-4-10. Now let's march back to the barracks. Company—attention!"

CHAPTER SEVENTEEN

Cindy Jones and Jack Boudreau met at a party—he a struggling reporter at the *Bangor Daily News*, and she a graduate student in English at the University of Maine. The party was hosted by a retiring history professor at UMaine, Professor Kohl, an expert on European intellectual history. Kohl invited faculty, staff, and current and former students of his at his home for hors d'oeuvres and cocktails.

The beautiful blond and blue-eyed Cindy caught Jack's eye immediately at the party, and the two quickly struck up a conversation. (Cindy would later confess that the only reason she gave Jack her phone number that night was because she was impressed with his knowledge of Alexis de Tocqueville's definitive work on America, *Democracy in America*.)

Jack and Cindy started dating shortly after Professor Kohl's party. The two often ate out, watched rented movies, and hung out with mutual friends at bookstores and bars that catered to the college crowd.

Both Cindy and Jack were content with their dating and relationship. Jack liked Cindy for her attractiveness and smarts; Cindy liked Jack solely for what she called his "potential"—his solid work ethic, ambition, and especially his interest in writing a novel and getting published.

But though content with the relationship, Jack started noticing differences between himself and his girlfriend soon after they became an "It," a "couple," a "going-steady couple."

The more he thought about these differences, the more he attributed them to different attitudes.

Probably culturally based attitudes, he thought.

Boudreau's thinking was: *My family's from Millinocket, a papermill town. Dad works at the mill; Mom works as a finance assistant for a local GMC truck dealership. Millinocket's a blue-collar town, solid Democrat. Dad's in a union, but he rarely votes for Democrats; Mom often votes for Democrats, but she'll crossover and vote Republican here and there. My family's middle class because of my dad's union job. Dad drives a GMC pickup; Mom a Chevrolet sedan. Family vacations when I grew up took place in Quebec, Canada, to visit relatives or to Old Orchard Beach to enjoy the sand and some lobsters. My family and I are Catholic.*

Cindy also grew up in a mill town— not a papermill town but a textile mill town, Waterville. But the Jones aren't millworkers. Cindy's dad teaches Russian history at Waterville's Colby College—a private and exclusive institution—while her mom runs a small art studio. The only reason Cindy chose UMaine for undergrad and grad school is because she got full scholarships to both. The Jones are Protestants. They drive Volvos. They vacation in Bar Harbor, Kennebunkport, and Europe, the latter where Professor Jones often does research. The Jones always vote Republican. My parents sometimes vote Republican, but they're Sam's Club Republicans; Cindy's family are country-club Republicans. The Jones actually do belong to a country club.

So there were differences between Cindy and Jack, and Jack viewed it as attitudinal and culturally-based. There were many examples of these differences, of course. Take art for example. Cindy liked art, especially Impressionist Art, but these things meant nothing to Jack because the fact was art wasn't something Jack knew or cared about. Then again, Jack's apartment walls were plastered with posters of athletes (mostly baseball players), a few writers (Hemingway and Maine's native son, Stephen King), and some of the great blues guitarists (B.B. King, Buddy Guy, and Stevie Ray Vaughan). Athletes, baseball, blues, and blues guitarists meant nothing to Cindy. She was, however, okay with posters of Hemingway and Stephen King.

So, Jack noticed these differences between himself and Cindy, and he was quite certain Cindy saw it the other way around too—the realization that: *My boyfriend, Jack, is different than me.*

One time, when Jack drove by a Bangor city street and remarked to Cindy: "That's a nice house for sale," Cindy quipped with, "Jack, that house for sale has a list price of $135,000 dollars. It ain't much of a house."

That time, right then and there, Jack thought to himself, *Wow, man. Boy, oh boy. Me and Cindy are sure different. I think it's a nice house, that $135,000 dollars buys you a nice house. Cindy thinks it ain't much of a house; that $135,000—a lot of money, I think—doesn't buy you a lot of house in Bangor. Boy oh boy.*

When Jack and Cindy's dating turned up a notch or two, Cindy decided (on her own) to move into Jack's apartment. Such a move had its ups and downs, its tradeoffs. More time together, living together—that was good. Cindy constantly on the phone talking to her girlfriends, actually spending less time with Jack—that was bad.

In all, Cindy's apartment move-in was short-lived because after only five weeks of living with Jack, she (once again on her own) decided to move in with a group of her girlfriends and share an apartment with them. Even while moving out, Cindy insisted—in fact she emphasized—that, "Jack, we're still a couple you know. We're still an 'It.'"

More differences, man, was Jack's reaction.

And then came Jack's untimely work cutback at the *Bangor Daily News*, which meant less pay, which meant moonlighting, which meant seeing less of Cindy. It also meant the need to realign goals and start looking at other options. In the end, it meant and brought about Jack's enlistment in the Army, and before he shipped out, Cindy, feeling vulnerable, sold the big C hard, the big Commitment, expressed in the form of an engagement symbolized by a diamond ring.

Jack knew there were differences between himself and Cindy, but he was convinced their relationship could work, that indeed it would work. But now, in those early days of Basic, when the daily Mail Call brought no letters from his fiancé, and all he heard on the receiving end of his nightly phone calls was the answering machine greeting, Jack Boudreau began to have some doubts about his engagement to Cindy Jones.

CHAPTER EIGHTEEN

Boudreau forced himself to take a break from Truman Capote's *In Cold Blood*. He took a bite from his blueberry muffin, and as he chewed he noticed more patrons entering the bookstore. He wiped his fingers with a napkin, then he glanced at his watch.

Carlos should be here in about two hours.

He leaned back in his chair and started thinking.

Well, if Carlos wants to meet me, then that's a sign my gut feelings were right all along.

He looked up at the wall in front of him, the wall depicting great writers like Faulkner, Hemingway, Shelley, Wilde, Steinbeck, Twain, and others. He thought some more:

The Boys figured I knew something, and I think they were after me. Yesterday, Carlos told me, 'We almost had you, J.B.' and 'Our plan was perfect.' Why would he say that? I'm sure they had a plan to get rid of me.

Boudreau took a sip of coffee. He looked out the front window of the Barnes & Noble and saw heavy pedestrian traffic.

I don't think I could have prevented any of this, he thought. *You know, it's my room too. Wasn't my fault I found out what The Boys were planning to do in that Taco Bell parking lot.*

He took another sip of coffee.

What could I have done differently? I faked it as best I could, but Boros probably figured I knew something. Maybe I could have hid in the room... nah, that wouldn't have saved me.

Hell man, all they had to do was lock the damn door. The damn door to my room was unlocked, which was strange because The Boys usually locked the door. My friggin' luck, man.

He shifted in his chair.

Yeah, The Boys knew I knew, and that's what Carlos wants to talk about this afternoon. Wonder what their game plan was to get rid of me, to get me kicked out of the Army.

He looked up at the ceiling, leaned back in his chair, and stretched his arms. Then he went back to reading *In Cold Blood.*

CHAPTER NINETEEN

Eyes burning and watery, snot dripping from his nose, an itchy face, a dry throat, a painful cough.

"How that gas shit feel, pukes?" asked Drill Sergeant Murdock. He was addressing a squad of recruits who had just exited one of the Basic Training gas chambers. Boudreau, who was one of the squad members, made sure not to rub his burning eyes because earlier the drill sergeants had said, "Don't rub y'all's burning eyes. Rubbing your eyes makes it worse."

Boudreau kept walking slowly. He was following the squad members ahead of him. The outdoor fresh air was actually a double sword for him. *Fresh air's good for my throat; I can now breathe. But the fresh air makes my face itchy and my eyes burn.*

"Drill Sergeant, with all due respect, the gas chamber made us feel like shit, drill sergeant." That was Carrington speaking. He too was one of the squad members who had just exited the small wooden cabin that served as the gas chamber.

"That's good," said Murdock as he spat some tobacco juice on the ground next to his boots. "Feeling like shit, heh? Hey, remember what I told you candy-ass recruits on the first day of Basic. 'Pain is good, right? Pain is just weakness leaving the body.'"

The squad consisted of Alvarez, Bodin, Carrington, Carey, Cassell, Bodette, Boudreau, and Brown. All were walking slowly to a clearing up ahead; all suffered from the same symptoms; all wanted to rub their burning eyes.

"Now I don't want any of y'all to get a case of the Chinese Disease," yelled Murdock as he followed the squad of recruits. "In case y'all are wondering, the Chinese Disease is Draggin' Ass or Dragon Ass—pick your fucking pronunciation. I want every one of y'all to follow the narrow trail to the open field. Once there, y'all see a big water barrel. That's y'all's cleaning solution to clean up your NBC Pro Masks. No ass-draggin' now, no Chinese Disease—keep it moving y'all."

The squad kept walking on the narrow trail and reached the cleaning barrel in less than three minutes. Murdock, standing next to the barrel, had his thick arms crossed over his chest. He was chewing his ever-present tobacco, and he made sure each recruit dipped their respective Pro Masks into the barrel containing the cleaning solution.

"I know the shit itches, y'all," he said as he opened a small white bottle of Motrin. He quickly popped one of the orange pills in his mouth. "Hmm—yummy. My Ranger candy still tastes good after all these years. Shit y'all, I've got fifty-eight jumps to my credit. Parachute down from a perfectly good flying plane fifty-eight times, and y'all too will have some back pain. Anyway, as I was saying, I know this CS gas shit itches like fuck, but the pain will go away in about another five mikes. Just suck it up and drive on, pukes."

The squad members started cleaning their chemical masks by gently wiping the cleaning solution from their masks; They used their Army-issued, brown-in-color handkerchief, to do the wiping.

"Gather 'round y'all," Murdock said. He gestured with his right hand. "Y'all gather 'round me next to this here barrel for a sec. Lemme tell y'all some tips 'bout this whole Basic Training thing."

The eight squad members did as instructed and formed a small circle around Murdock.

"All right, y'all. Y'all are a pretty-squared-away squad so stay that way," Murdock said matter-of-factly. He pulled out a pack of Marlboros and quickly placed a cigarette between his lips. "This Basic Training thing is too easy privates, too easy. All y'all gotta do is follow orders. Just don't be zigging when we tell y'all to zag. Once in a while there's a little pain— like this gas chamber training—but overall, it ain't too bad. Remember—follow orders; drink the Kool Aid."

He quickly lit the cigarette and took a puff.

"And where there's pain—well, we say FIDO, right?—Fuck It, Drive On." He exhaled the cigarette smoke. "Suck it up like a man, like a soldier. Life will give you some speed bumps, and so will this Basic Training thing, but just about everyone here will graduate. Fact is fellas, the pukes who don't graduate from Basic are pukes who got themselves an injury or they've got attitude problems. Broke dicks and wusses are the ones who can't cut it in Basic. Take care of yourselves, fellas. Especially take care of your feet when we start those road marches. And take care of your battle buddies. And don't make any excuses, right?"

"Hooah," replied the squad members. Murdock smiled. He took another puff. He exhaled.

"Hey y'all, what's the maximum effective range of an excuse? Zero, right? We don't make excuses. Soldiers don't make excuses. A little pain? Just FIDO it. Never be a wuss."

"Hooah," replied the squad members.

"Y'all will have fun later this afternoon when we do the pugil-stick fighting. That'll be some of the most fun y'all will have in Basic. Now, before I release you ladies to clean your masks some more, any of y'all know what a twat is? That's the question of the day. What's a twat, Second Squad of First Platoon? C'mon now."

Carey burst out laughing as the other recruits smiled. Murdock was also smiling.

"C'mon, anyone? What's a twat?"

Carrington, standing directly to Murdock's left, cleared his throat and said, "Well drill sergeant, a twat is the female—"

"No, no, Carrington," Murdock said, cutting him off in mid-sentence. "Your mind's in the gutter, son. I order you to open mouth and insert foot—no no, just kidding. Open mouth and insert foot is Army talk for shut the fuck up. Anyway, not that twat, Carrington. See y'all, a twat is a Tanker Without a Tank. I was once in the armor branch so I know all 'bout tanks. My grandpa was a tanker too. He was in the Big One—World War II. Fought the damn Germans in Africa and Europe. Fuckin' Krauts had better tanks than we did. Tells y'all what, you didn't want to be a twat in that war."

CHAPTER TWENTY

J ose Gonzalez and Carlos Rivera had much in common: they both grew up in San Antonio, Texas; they both quit high school and later got GEDs; they both loved to work on cars; they both hated their fathers and loved their mothers; and they both signed up with the Army, did their Basic Training together, and got assigned to the same duty station.

Of the two, Jose had been the first to sign up with the Army. Actually, it was four months prior to Basic Training that Jose first met Carlos at a party, where the two struck a conversation that at one point brought up questions about Jose's recent Army enlistment.

How much does it pay?

How hard will Basic Training be?

You get thirty days paid vacation—for real?

The G.I. Bill can be used for Votech training? Is that right?

You have to run two miles in about seventeen minutes?

Such were the many questions Carlos had fired in Jose's direction, and toward the end of the party, Jose gave the curious Carlos his Army recruiter's business card.

"Give the recruiter a call, Carlos. He'll answer all your questions."

"I may just do that," an enthused Carlos replied. "Fact is, I wouldn't mind getting money to get Votech training. I really like working on my car, man. Right now I'm giving it a new paint job, and then I plan on replacing the mag wheels."

* * *

Four weeks later, Jose got a phone call while he was munching on a sandwich in his mother's kitchen.

"Congratulations, Mr. Gonzalez."

Puzzled, Jose answered, "Who is this?"

"This is Sergeant Marquez, your recruiter."

"Oh, hello, hello sergeant," replied Jose, slightly embarrassed he hadn't recognized the voice.

"Sergeant, I'm all pumped up about my upcoming Basic Training. I'm jogging every day, and I'm working on my push-ups too."

"Well, I'm happy to hear that, stud," said Marquez, an eight-year Army veteran. "And I've got some good news for you, too."

"What's that, sergeant? What's the good news?"

"Well high-speed, I got here a check in your name for fifty bucks."

"Cool," replied an even more enthused Jose. "But why the money? What did I do for it?"

"Well stud, you referred a friend of yours to me, a Carlos Rivera. I just signed him up today, and we have this Army referral policy where we give fifty bucks for a referral."

"Ah, that's cool, sergeant," Jose said. He got up from his chair and started walking around his Mom's kitchen.

"Yeah, me and Carlos have been hanging out a bit. I just met the dude 'bout a month ago. We now work on cars together and shit. He told me he was thinking 'bout signing up. So he did, huh?"

"That's right, he signed up," said Marquez. "And guess what? As much as he wanted to be a mechanic, I signed him up for Supply just like you because the Army's got enough mechanics right now but we need more Supply clerks. It wouldn't surprise me at all if you two did training together."

"Hey, that's cool, sergeant."

And so it was—the two recent buddies from San Antonio enlisted in the Army, did their military training together, and ended up both being stationed at Fort Leavenworth, Kansas. And once there, they had something else in common: they both started transporting drugs for Specialist Dustin Boros.

CHAPTER TWENTY-ONE

"This afternoon, we'll find out who the real recruits are," said Drill Sergeant Collinsworth. He was addressing the three-company C-4-10 formation in the middle of a large grass field. Thunder was rumbling, dark clouds were visible from the west, and a faint drizzle was falling.

"Pugil-stick fighting is a perfect complement to this morning's gas chamber adventures if you ask me. Now I know it's raining a bit, and you know what I'm gonna tell you bunch of wusses—suck it up and drive on! Shit, back when I was with the 82nd Airborne Division, we used to say, 'If it ain't raining, we ain't training.' Just suck it up, pukes. Rain won't kill y'all. Tracking?"

"Hooah," replied the 120 members of the company.

"Right on Charlie-4-10, that's what I'm talking about," said Collinsworth, all smiles. He paused for a second or two, then he said, "Now lemme tell you all a coupla tips on pugil-stick fighting. One, if you're on defense in this business, you're in trouble. The key is to be on offense, to keep attacking and hitting your opponent. Two, always face your opponent—never have your back to him. Look at your opponent and attack. Remember—stay alert, stay alive. Everyone tracking?"

"Hooah," replied the company of recruits.

"Good," said Collinsworth. "Now, pair up with some other puke from your platoon. On my command of fall out, fall out and pair up with some puke who weighs about the same as you do. Drill Sergeant Moran will be the referee. Weather forecast says the skies will clear up, and the grass ain't too wet right now so we're good to go. Good luck everyone. Go out there and kick some you know what. Fallout!"

The formation broke up, and soon after, Boudreau noticed a heap of equipment behind Collinsworth. He saw face masks and gloves like the ones hockey players wear, and chest protectors like those worn by baseball catchers. And then he noticed the pugil sticks themselves—five-foot-long plastic sticks resembling cotton swab Q-tips.

Well I just hope I don't embarrass myself out here, he thought as he started walking toward the pile of equipment. Then he started thinking: who can I pair up with? *Bodette's over two hundred pounds—Bodin? Bodin weights about the same as I do—oh, but I see he's paired up with Carrera. Hmmn? Who's about my size?*

He kept walking toward the equipment, then he suddenly heard—

"J.B., got a partner?"

Boudreau turned around and saw that it was Cassell.

"No, you looking for one?" asked Boudreau.

"Roger, I don't have a fight partner yet," said Cassell. "Whaddaya say?"

Boudreau figured Cassell weighed about the same as he did even though Cassell was taller.

"I'd say you're my pugil-stick opponent."

* * *

Ten minutes later, Boudreau and Cassell were being assisted with putting on the protective gear for their upcoming battle.

"Cassell's a lefty, J.B., so watch those blows coming from the left," Bodette told his battle buddy as he helped him put on the chest protector. Cassell was being assisted by Bodin.

"And Collinsworth's right about that offensive stuff. Don't be looking to block blows and shit. Just keep swinging. The only round I lost to Harrison was the one I wasn't aggressive enough."

"Okay, roger," said Boudreau, nodding his head.

"And keep your head up," said Bodette as he snapped Boudreau's facemask chinstrap. "Action's fast, buddy. Better keep your eyes open."

"Got it," said Boudreau, feeling some butterflies in his stomach.

"And your BCGs are on tight? Don't want 'em glasses slipping and shit."

"Roger," said Boudreau. "I got my eyeglass straps on."

"All right," said Bodette. "Good luck, man. Remember—keep swinging."

"Got it."

Less than a minute later came the sound of a loud whistle. "Next!" yelled Drill Sergeant Moran. He was standing in the middle of the grass field. Boudreau and Cassell walked together toward Moran.

"Good luck," said Cassell. "May the best man, win."

"Same goes," said Boudreau. He was still nervous, but the walking seemed to help curb his butterflies.

"Okay you two, here's how it works," said Moran when the pair reached him. "Both of you line up backside to backside. When I blow the whistle, you guys take ten paces forward without looking at each other. After the ten paces, turn around, and go after your opponent—you two can rumble. Best two out of three rounds takes it. Once the fighting starts, the cue for who won that particular round will be my whistle again, so if you hear my whistle during the fight, stop fighting. It means I've declared a winner for the round."

Both Boudreau and Cassell said nothing.

"Okay," said Moran. "Touch sticks and may the best puke win."

Boudreau and Cassell lined up backside to backside. Moran blew the whistle, and the two warriors started walking in opposite directions.

Five paces, six paces, seven, counted Boudreau to himself. He quickly counted ten paces, turned around, and saw that Cassell was rushing toward him.

Christ. Stay stationary? Attack? His mind was racing.

What do I do? Cassell was closing in.

Forget defense—attack!

Boudreau started slow-jogging toward Cassell. Cassell, still rushing in, was holding his pugil stick high, telegraphing a big overhand blow.

Bam! Cassell's pugil stick struck Boudreau's stick and the top portion of Boudreau's facemask.

Where is he? Where is he? Boudreau thought.

He glanced to his rear and saw that Cassell's momentum had carried him seven paces away. Boudreau quickly turned around. Cassell was again rushing him and preparing another overhand blow.

Another loud *bam* when the pugil sticks collided. Cassell started swinging short strokes and jabs, all coming from his left side. Boudreau in defensive mode did his best to fend off blows.

Damn it. I know I won't win by being defensive.

More short blows from Cassell, then an opening when he missed widely and lost his footing. Boudreau realized that Cassell's backside was facing him, so he took two short stabs with his pugil stick to Cassell's back. Cassell replied by swinging and eventually standing up. Back and forth it went—Boudreau with short jabs, short strokes; Cassell with blocking strokes and the occasional overhand blow. At one point, the two locked sticks, and that's when Cassell braced his back left leg for better balance and pushed Boudreau back two paces.

Then, more exchanges—Cassell's blows always generated from his left side; Boudreau swinging short jabs and trying not to back up. Suddenly, a *paw-thump*—a clean overhand blow from Cassell connected squarely with Boudreau's facemask.

Shit, thought Boudreau. He bent his knees to improve his balance, and he started a counterblow of his own but then the whistle blew.

The two opponents started walking back in the direction of Moran.

"Good round, J.B.," Cassell said, winded.

"You too," said Boudreau. He too was breathing heavily. "Think you got me on that one."

"Round one to the southpaw," yelled Moran in a commanding voice once the two arrived at the center of the field. Some "Go Cassell" and "C'mon J.B.s" could be heard from the First Platoon recruits on the sidelines. The two lined up again—backside-to-backside. Moran blew the whistle, and the pair each counted off ten paces.

Boy, I can't afford to lose another round, thought Boudreau as he counted off his paces. *Need to win two rounds in a row. Focus. Focus.*

He noticed he didn't have butterflies in his stomach anymore. He turned around. Cassell was walking (not rushing) in his direction. More blows—Cassell's again always coming from his left side. Boudreau, knowing he had to *show more offense,* made a conscious decision to keep moving forward even if it meant he sustained some blows. And it worked because Cassell was now constantly backing up, which made it difficult for him to wind up with his favored overhand blows.

More exchanges, with Boudreau moving forward and Cassell backpeddling. Then, Boudreau missed widely with a side blow, the momentum of which exposed his unprotected back to Cassell.

I can't see Cassell, but I bet he's coming after me. Fuck it.

Boudreau swung blindly with a roundhouse blow in Cassell's direction. *Paw-thump.* The blow connected with Cassell's chest protector. Then the whistle blew.

Man, I lucked out on that one, Boudreau thought as he and Cassell headed toward Moran. *Swung with my back to my opponent. Lucky I connected.*

"Good round, J.B.," Cassell said. He was winded and breathing heavy. "Think you got me."

"Maybe I did; who knows?" replied Boudreau, also winded.

He thought: *at least I'm not embarrassing myself out here.*

"Round two to the righty," Moran declared, tapping Boudreau's facemask as the two fighters reached the drill sergeant. "We have ourselves a cheese match, First Platoon."

More "Go Cassell" and "C'mon J.B.s" from the sidelines.

"All right, you two; good fighting," Moran said as he instructed the pair to line up again backside-to-backside. "Count your ten paces, and fight this last and decisive round."

Stay on offense, Boudreau reminded himself as he counted off his paces. His BCG glasses felt looser around his head, and they were fogged up a bit, but he was confident they'd hold up. *Stay focused. Stay on offense. Just one more round. This will be over soon.*

He turned around. He saw Cassella turn around too. Boudreau picked up a slow jog, as did Cassell.

Bam! The two pugil sticks collided. Blows exchanged. Boudreau tried to move forward, but Cassell put on too much pressure. Boudreau heard background noises and cheers, but he couldn't make them out because he was focused on Cassell's face and facemask. More exchange of blows; close up fighting; Cassell's and Boudreau's feet inches apart, sometimes touching.

Boudreau tried to shove Cassell back, but Cassell's feet and balance were dead on and he hardly moved. Boudreau again tried to push off Cassell, and this time Cassell took two steps backward, which prompted Boudreau to immediately come with an overhand right—it actually just missed Cassell's right shoulder. Cassell, with his feet wide apart, countered with a short left jab to Boudreau's right-side ribs. The blow landed and pushed Boudreau back, and that's when Cassell lunged forward, but he missed with an overhand blow. More exchanges. More pressure from Cassell. Boudreau, thinking he'd get better balance if he took a couple steps backward, started backing up, but he slipped on the wet grass, and then the next thing he knew Cassell was on top of him. More exchanges, but they were strictly defensive blocks by Boudreau. Then, the sound of Moran's whistle.

Damn it. Why did I back up? thought Boudreau. *I know I lost this last round.*

He was tired. He stood up, and as he did he caught a glimpse of Cassell who was smiling and pumping his right arm in the air as a sign of victory. Boudreau started walking toward Moran to hear the final verdict. For the first time, he realized his forearms were tight and sore from all the exchange of blows.

Well I did my best, he thought as he heard Moran declare Cassell the winner. *At least I didn't embarrass myself out here this morning.*

CHAPTER TWENTY-TWO

That evening, at around 2000 hours, Boudreau was in one of the five phone booths adjacent to the barracks. The only mail he had received thus far in the first two weeks of Basic were two letters from his parents—no letters from Cindy and no phone conversations either, because each time he had called her he'd gotten the answering machine. He was hoping he'd have better luck tonight.

He called the number to their Bangor apartment. A pick up after the third ring.

"Hello?"

"Cindy, it's me—Jack."

"Oh, hi Jack. How's it going?"

"Good, I'm doing good. Heh, I've called almost every night and I keep getting the answering machine."

"Uh, yeah—well, I've been busy lately, yunno."

He paused. There was brief silence. "Well, today we did this gas chamber training—it wasn't easy let me tell you. Then we had a pugil-stick competition. I didn't win, but I fought okay."

"Oh, that's nice," said Cindy. Her tone was unenthused.

"So you doing okay, Cin?"

"Yeah, yeah, everything's fine. Volvo's still making noise, but yunno how it is."

"Yeah. Heh, I miss you, Cin."

"Yeah, me too." Then a short pause. "Uh, Jack, me and the girls are going out tonight. Lisa's driving. I gotta go. Miss y'a. Kisses." Then a click.

Chapter Twenty-Three

"Charlie-4-10, today's the big day," said Drill Sergeant Murdock. He was speaking to the entire company, which had assembled on wooden bleachers adjacent to Range Seven. A thin, protruding metal roof served as the bleachers' overhang and provided shade from the sun. It was ten AM, and C-4-10 was exactly at the midway point of their eight-week Basic Training. Murdock, who was sporting dark sunglasses, was standing next to the lowest level of bleachers. He looked up at the recruits as he spoke.

"Today's Q-day, pukes. Qualification Day—a necessary part of Basic Training," he said as he spat his ever-present tobacco juice spit on the ground.

"Now, I know y'all are hot and wearing your battle rattle—K-pot, pistol belt, ammo pouches, two canteens, and your Pro Mask in its case. That equipment's making y'all hotter. Well tough shit. FIDO, pukes. Fuck It, Drive On. Just make sure y'all drink plenty of water this morning. I don't want any of y'all dehydrated when you're qualifying with your M16." He paused for just a second, spat tobacco juice on the ground again, then said, "Range NCO will get this range fired up shortly, then we'll get the first firing order going. This is just like y'alls BRM marksmanship training pukes. See pop-up target, hit pop-up target. Twenty-three out of forty hits qualifies your sorry asses. Remember Drill Sergeant Collinsworth's two tips. One, always know your SPORTS because you don't know if and when a malfunction will occur. S stands for what now?"

"Slap," answered the nervous recruits.

"That's right," said Murdock. "Slap the magazine. P stands for what?"

"Pull," replied the recruits.

"Right, pull the charging handle. O stands for what now?"

"Observe," answered the recruits in unison.

"Right," said Murdock. "Observe the chamber. And R stands for?"

"Release," replied the C-4-10 recruits.

"Correct," Murdock said. "Release the charging handle. You dumbfucks aren't so fucking dumb after all. And T stands for what now?"

"Tap," replied the recruits.

"That's right," answered Murdock. He spat on the ground again. "Tap the forward assist. And what does the last S in SPORTS stand for?"

"Squeeze," replied C-4-10.

"Right again," said Murdock. "Squeeze the fucking trigger and hope your weapon ain't malfunctioning."

Murdock crossed his thick arms across his chest. "And the second tip from Drill Sergeant Collinsworth was the one about missing low if y'all gonna miss. Remember that one?"

"Hooah," replied the nervous and anxious recruits.

"If you're running out of time and you're in a hurry to shoot a target and your aim is jacked up like a fucking goat rope soup sandwich thing, then it's better to aim too low then it is to aim too high, right? Just like Drill Sergeant Collinsworth said about baseball: if you know you've got to rush to throw the ball to the first baseman, it's better to throw too low then it is to throw too high. Throw the ball twenty feet above the first baseman, and he ain't got a prayer; throw the ball to him in the dirt and he's got a chance at scooping it up. Same thing with firing at a target, pukes. Gotta rush your aim, aim on the low side. You aim too high y'all miss the target every time; aim a bit too low, and you never know if the bullet will strike the ground in front of the target and kick some dirt or a rock or both with enough force to strike down the pop-up target and record it as a hit. Everyone tracking?"

"Hooah," replied the recruits.

"All righty then," said Murdock. "Good luck, pukes. And for you sorry asses who don't qualify, we'll place your sorry asses in a special firing order and give you more ammo till y'all qualify. Good luck Charlie-4-10. Go out there and kick some butt this morning. Oh, and by the way, y'all are exactly halfway done with Basic Training."

"Hooah," replied the recruits loudly.

"Oh and because y'all's been a pretty good company, then we high-speed drill sergeants are now letting y'all drink caffeinated drinks like sodas and coffee."

An even louder "Hooah" from the recruits followed that comment from Murdock.

"Now don't abuse this caffeine thing, y'all. Sodas got a lot of sugar in 'em. Some of you fat candy asses still need to slim down for your final graded PT test. We all tracking?"

"Hooah," replied the recruits.

"Okay, good," said Murdock. He quickly spat tobacco juice on the ground again. "Again, good luck pukes. Remember—see target, hit target."

Boudreau was sitting four rows back in the bleachers. Sitting to his right was his battle buddy, Bodette; to his immediate left was Bodin. Throughout the previous two weeks of BRM (basic rifle marksmanship), Boudreau and the other members of Second Squad, First Platoon, had always been placed in the first firing order. Boudreau figured Q-day would be no different, and based on that, he figured his firing order would be called up in about half an hour.

I'm nervous, man, he thought to himself as he contemplated the morning's task of qualifying with his M16. *Got those butterflies again.*

Chapter Twenty-Four

Most of the C-4-10 recruits were nervous because qualifying with the M16, though not the most difficult of tasks, wasn't exactly a cake walk either because they actually had to produce results; they actually had to shoot down the requisite number of targets—at least twenty-three out of a possible forty to be exact. Then, add the fact that their M16s could malfunction, and you've got yourself a bit of a pressure-cooker/stressful situation. Plus, Boudreau's shooting performance during the two-week BRM was so-so at best, so that too played to his nervousness.

I'll take marksman, he told himself while waiting in the bleachers. *Sharpshooter would be nice, but I'll take marksman. Expert is really out of my league.*

Beside his so-so M16 shooting, however, certain things had gone fairly well for Boudreau during his previous two weeks of BRM. PT was one such gone-fairly-well thing—very well in fact, because after four weeks of Basic, Boudreau found himself with the third-highest PT score in the entire 120-member company. Push-ups were his best event. He could do seventy-eight of them within the two-minute time limit, and his two-mile run time of slightly over thirteen minutes was also decent for his age group. Sit-ups was his worst exercise in the three-event PT test, but even that (sixty-eight sit-ups in two minutes) was a very solid score. Still, the competitive Boudreau vowed to improve on his two-minute sit-up count, and he also vowed to do his very best for the final PT test and stay in the running for the top PT award.

And then there was the whole routine of Basic Training—that too had gone well for Boudreau: up early out of bed; polish the boots; wear the uniform; breakfast chow; pick up one's M16; cattle truck drive to a firing range; fire the M16; outdoor lunch at the firing range; fire the M16 again; march back to barracks or sometimes cattle-truck ride to the barracks; change into PT uniform; do PT (alternate between run days versus push-up/sit-up days); shower; dinner chow; clean barracks; Mail Call; phone privileges; do laundry if need be; lights out at 2200. That was the routine Monday through Saturday, and Boudreau had no problems with it. On Sundays—a day off from training—he would attend Catholic Mass, and then, he'd mow lawns and pick up weeds like the other recruits. He also would catch up on laundry and get a haircut.

Overall, Boudreau liked the routine of Basic Training. He did miss TV (especially ESPN, C-SPAN, and *The Tonight Show with Jay Leno*), and he did miss books and newspapers, but again, overall, he had no problems with the Basic Training routine. And now, Murdock had just recently said that caffeine—to include coffee—was no longer prohibited, so that too was another plus.

But then there was the Cindy issue. Cindy. That wasn't going so well. Boudreau's almost-daily phone calls nearly always ended up as messages on the answering machine, and when he did finally reach Cindy, there was very little conversation from her. No "I miss you," no "I love you." Just quick polite conversation that almost always ended with Cindy saying, "Gotta go. Bye." And no letters from Cindy either.

CHAPTER TWENTY-FIVE

Boudreau took another break from reading Truman Capote's *In Cold Blood*. He had first read Capote's great work two years prior, and now his second reading was just as pleasant and enjoyable as his first.

Boy, Capote could write, he thought. He quickly glanced at his watch. It read 2:12.

Less than two hours till I meet Carlos— the afternoon is going by fast. Kinda of thirsty right now. I might as well get in line now for a bottle of water 'cause the line never seems to get shorter.

He stood up and got in line with the other numerous patrons, but he brought his copy of *In Cold Blood* just to browse through and keep himself occupied. He started thumbing through the book and skimming the passages:

It was inexplicable, and he turned to leave, but he turned again and wondered toward the house—white and solid and spacious. He had always been impressed by it, and pleased to think that his girlfriend lived there. But now that it was deprived of the late owner's dedicated attention, the first threads of decay's cob web were being spun. A gravel rake lay rusting in the driveway; the lawn was parched and shabby ...

Boy Capote sure could write, he thought as he slowly moved up the waiting line. *Incredible stuff. You know, Norman Mailer was right when he said Truman Capote writes the best sentences. What a phrase, what a great sentence to describe a house falling in disrepair – "the first strings of decay's cob web were being spun"'* Wow. Awesome. I've never read a better writer than Truman Capote.

Boudreau kept moving forward towards the Starbucks ordering line, and he kept skimming through *In Cold Blood*.

I sure hope Carlos clears things up for me. Shit man, I still think I did the best I could. It was less than two weeks ago. It was a Wednesday night – I remember it was a Wednesday because Wednesday is when we stay late at the office to do the layout of the Lamp newspaper. I got to my barracks room around 8 PM, and as I was walking down the barracks hallway I heard loud music coming from my room. I figured Boros and his Boys were in the room doing their usual— smoking cancer sticks and drinking brewskies. Heck, it was my room too, man, not just Boros's room, even though he was my roommate at the time. I entered my room—it was strange that the door wasn't locked, but again, it's my room, too. I enter my room and that's when I heard their plans to—

"What will it be, sir? —Sir, your order?" asked the Starbucks employee working the cash register.

Boudreau, daydreaming about that fateful evening, did a double take. "Uh, uh, I'll have a bottle of water please. And, and—" he glanced to his right to look at the attractive pastry shelves. "And also an oatmeal-raisin cookie."

"Bottle of water and a cookie, coming right up," said the cashier.

Chapter Twenty-Six

"I'm Sergeant First Class Rollins, the NCOIC, noncommissioned officer in charge, of this range. This morning is Qualification Day, Charlie-4-10," said the tall, heavy-set black NCO who was standing in front of the bleachers. His voice was surprisingly soft for a big man.

"This is just like BRM, except today it counts. Now, a coupla things to cover. One, everyone here is a safety officer. You see something unsafe, stop what you're doing and tell your nearest range safety what unsafe act you see. I'll have four range safeties spread out with each firing order, and each range safety is also an NCO, so they've been around some and know what they're doing. Two, always follow my commands, which I'll be giving from the range tower. Three, as you all know, there's plenty of wildlife here in these surrounding woods. We've got deer and turkeys especially. Don't be Rambo out here and shoot at the wildlife. Just leave the wildlife alone. Four, water buffalo is behind these covered bleachers, so if you need to fill up your canteens with water that's where you need to go—the big water buffalo metal tank. Also, if you need to take a dump or drain the main vein, then we have two heads here. We have two Porta Johns some fifty meters to the east of these bleachers. Everybody tracking?"

"Hooah," replied the C-4-10 recruits while they still sat in the bleachers.

"Good," said Rollins. "Now I know this qualification stuff is nerve-wracking as fuck for most of you. I know it's tough to push the noodle up the flagpole, but you just gotta do your best. That's all you can do—do your best. In the last two weeks, we've shown y'all how to suck the egg. We've shown you the basic principles of marksmanship. Keep those principles in mind, Charlie-4-10, and good luck to all of you. Lemme have the first two firing orders."

The First Platoon recruits of C-4-10, including Boudreau, stood up and formed two horizontal lines in front of the bleachers. In less than five minutes they were all issued two twenty-round magazines from an NCO occupying a small wooden shed that served as the ammo point.

"Range walk, range walk to your foxholes first firing order," ordered Rollins through the range-tower PA system. "And put on your earplugs."

Please Lord, no malfunctions this morning, Boudreau prayed as he followed the other recruits to his designated foxhole. *I gotta pass this qualification thing.* He felt butterflies again in his stomach. *Remember—steady aim, controlled breathing, proper trigger squeeze. I just need to qualify.*

Boudreau followed the firing order line and ended up with foxhole twelve. Once there, he immediately placed his M16 on the short wooden weapons stand to the right of the foxhole. Next, he placed his two magazines on the small green felt square underneath the weapon's stand, and then he carefully stepped down into his four-foot deep foxhole.

"Okay firers, make yourselves comfortable in your foxholes," ordered Rollins from the range tower. His voice was loud and clear from the amplifying PA system. "Make sure the sandbags are the way you like them."

Boudreau, standing on a wooden pallet that served as the foxhole's floor, removed the top sandbag from the ground in front of him and placed it to his left, out of his view. He then grabbed his M16 with his right hand and placed his left hand—palm up—on the top of the other sandbag directly in front of him.

Left hand guides the barrel, right hand on hand grip, he reminded himself. He started looking down range of Lane Twelve.

"Okay firers, this is a test run," said Rollins. "Watch your lane and ensure you see every target. The targets will stay up for the same amount of time as if you're firing."

Yep, I see the two fifty-meter targets—two plastic, green, torso targets. And there's the hundred- meter target ...and the two 150s ...the 200 ...the 250-meter target ...oh, and that tiny thing out there, that's the 300-meter target. Nah, man, I ain't firing at you this morning, thought Boudreau as he looked down Lane Twelve. *Haven't hit you during the two weeks of BRM, so I don't think I'll hit you this morning. I'm gonna keep those rounds for easier targets.*

Boudreau kept looking down his lane. Both to the left and to the right of the lane he noticed short wooden white signs with the number 12 on them.

Nice range, he thought. *Nice lanes. Sunny and clear weather too. Hardly any wind. No excuses if I don't qualify today. What's the maximum effective range of an excuse? Answer: zero. No excuses—I better qualify.*

"Okay firers, go ahead and lock-and-load a twenty-round magazine in your weapon," ordered Rollins from the Range Tower. "And assume a good prone-supported firing position."

Boudreau, like the other firers, did as ordered.

Fucking butterflies, man. I'm guessing they'll go away once I start firing.

Rollins said, "Are we clear on the right?" and two NCOs serving as range safeties waved short wooden paddles with the white side of the paddle facing Rollins.

"We're clear on the right. Clear on the left? No, I see red," said Rollins as one of the range safeties to the left waved his paddle with the red-side facing Rollins. "We are not clear on the left. Firer sixteen needs assistance."

A range safety NCO quickly walked up to firer sixteen and assisted him with his weapon. Boudreau couldn't make out who firer sixteen was. He took a deep breath and tried to remain calm.

Won't be long now.

"Okay, we're now clear on the left," said Rollins.

Boudreau, nervous with butterflies, kept looking down his lane.

Each pop-up target has a small dirt mound in front of it, he reminded himself. *And I generally know the order of the targets. Steady aim, proper breathing, good trigger squeeze. I gotta qualify, man.*

"Firers, assume a good prone position. Switch your selector lever from safe to semi, and watch your lane."

Dead silence. Then, the two fifty-meter targets—one to the left, the other to the right— popped up. His M16 made its pah-pah sound.

I hit them; I know I hit them both Boudreau thought to himself. *I better hit them since they're the easiest, but they don't stay up for too long.*

Pah-pah-pah sounds came from some of the other firers. Then silence, then the hundred-meter silhouette target popped up. Boudreau fired. The pah sound of the M16. The target went down.

Boudreau, with his left eye closed, his right eye open, and the tip of his nose resting on the edge of his M16's charging handle, looked down his lane with the open right eye.

Steady aim, man. Steady aim. I think the next target to go up is the 200-meter one, not the 150s.

Silence. Three seconds passed, then the 200-meter target popped up. Boudreau squeezed the trigger. The target stayed up.

Damn it.

He squeezed the trigger again. The target went down.

Not much harm done, he thought. *I won't fire at the 300-meter target anyway, so I can afford a second shot on some other targets.*

More targets popping up. Boudreau, shifting his aim accordingly, zeroed in and fired as best he could. And true to his strategy, he didn't fire at the farthest target, the 300-meter.

More targets popped up. More pah-pah sounds as he fired his M16.

I think I'm doing okay, he thought. *Missed a 200 and a 150, but I'm doing okay.*

The 300-meter target popped up again.

No thanks, thought Boudreau. *Gonna skip on that bad boy.*

Then the 150-meter target stood up.

Aim and fire. Pah—a hit. The 200—*aim and fire.* Another hit. The hundred-meter target. Boudreau fired and saw it too go down.

Good, doing good, he thought.

Then one of the 150-meter targets popped up. *Aim and fire.* The pah sound, and the target stayed up. *Damn it.* He fired again. The green plastic torso target went down.

More targets, more hits for Boudreau. Then suddenly the two 50-meter targets went up. Boudreau shifted to the left, fired, and hit the left-side target. He immediately shifted to the right, he aimed and squeezed the trigger and—click.

What the—?

He fired again. Again the mechanical clicking sound. The target went down on its own.

Shit, I ran out of ammo— that's the click sound, man. Oh well, I think I fired okay.

"Seize fire, seize fire," Rollins yelled over the PA system. "Firers, remove your magazines, lock your bolts to the rear, place your weapons on safe, and place your weapon on the rack. Once you've executed these commands, please stand up."

Boudreau followed the instructions, but before placing his M16 on the rack he made sure to observe the weapon's chamber to see if any rounds were in there. He also checked the magazine itself for rounds. There were no leftover rounds. He placed his M16 on the weapons' rack, and then he stood up.

"Okay firers, exit your foxholes and assume a good prone unsupported position next to your weapon," ordered Rollins.

Boudreau, like the other firers, got down on his belly.

I always fire better from the prone unsupported, he thought. *Stomach on the ground, elbows also on the ground. God, I hope I qualify. I think I did well. Twenty-three hits to qualify.*

"Firers, lock and load a twenty-round magazine. Are we clear on the right? We are clear on the right," said Rollins from the Range Tower. "Are we clear on the left? We are clear on the left. Firers, move your selector lever from safe to semi, and watch your lane."

Targets popping up, the pah-pah sounds of the M16. Boudreau aimed at the popping-up targets and fired accordingly.

This will all be over in two minutes, he thought. *Need twenty-three hits to qualify.*

The 200-meter target popped up. Boudreau aimed and fired. The target went down. The two 150-meter targets were next. From what Boudreau could tell he hit both.

I'm shooting well—see target, hit target. Steady aim, proper trigger squeeze.

More targets, more hits by Boudreau's estimation. The hundred-meter target sprung up. Boudreau squeezed the trigger. The pah sound of his M16. The target stayed up.

C'mon now.

He fired again. The silhouette target disappeared behind the dirt mound.

I think I got it—hmm? Maybe it dropped on its own.

More targets. More pah-pah-pah sounds. Then, the 300-meter target appeared.

Nah, man, I'm keeping my strategy. Plus, I want bullets left for my last fifty-meter targets unlike my previous firing round.

More targets, more hits. The occasional miss—he missed a 250-meter and a 100-meter.

Still doing well. See target, hit target.

Then the 300-meter target again. Boudreau stared at it. *Boy that sucker stays up long. Ah what the hell,* he thought. *I'm firing well—I got a shot at this.* He carefully aimed and checked his breathing. *It's all in the trigger squeeze,* he thought. He gingerly squeezed the trigger, the M16's pah sound resulted, and the target went down.

All right, cowboy. Hotdamn. Got me a 300.

More targets, more hits, then he missed a 200-meter. And then the two fifty-meter targets.

This is it—the last targets. He quickly shifted to the left, aimed, and fired. A hit. He immediately aimed his weapon to the right, quickly aimed, and fired. The result was the metallic click sound.

Damn it, out of ammo again. Oh well, I know those were the last targets because—

"Seize fire, seize fire," ordered Rollins. "Firers, remove your magazines, lock your bolts to the rear, and place your weapons on safe. Then crack open y'all's weapons to get rodded. Pick up all your stuff, and range walk to the ammo shed to get rodded, now. Range walk firers, get a move on and range walk."

* * *

Less than ten minutes later, Boudreau was lined up along with his twenty-member firing order. Facing the line of recruits was the C-4-10 company commander, Captain Hudson, an officer the company hardly saw thus far in Basic. Boudreau, holding his M16 by his side with the butt touching the ground ever so slightly, had his right index and middle fingers crossed for good luck.

"Okay, good firing, gentlemen," Hudson said in a clear voice. "You all qualified."

Whew, thought Boudreau. *Thank you, Jesus.* Many of the other recruits were also relieved. Bodette and Carrington actually high-fived each other.

Hudson began to individually shake hands and personally congratulate each firer. He also handed out the appropriate medal—marksman, sharpshooter, or expert—and told each firer his respective score.

"Carrington, thirty two, congratulations, son, that's sharpshooter; Bodin, good job, twenty eight, that's marksman; Carey, twenty three, marksman. You squeezed in there son, and keep working on those push-ups; Brown, twenty five, also marksman. Good job. Cassell, thirty five. You just missed expert by one, high-speed. That's sharpshooter. Baker, congrats stud, you hit thirty-seven targets, good for expert. Well done. Bodette, good job. You got thirty. Boudreau, good job. You hit thirty one—"

CHAPTER TWENTY-SEVEN

Boudreau returned to his corner table at the Barnes &
Noble bookstore. He sat down and started chewing on his
oatmeal raisin cookie.

*Yeah, I don't know if I could've done anything different that
night. I'm guessing Boros figured I knew something was up.
That's what Carlos wants to talk about.*

He took a sip of water, then his thoughts changed to …
*Capote's inspiring me. When I first got here this afternoon, I
was in no mood to work on that novel of mine. But now, after
reading some of Capote's* In Cold Blood, *I feel like writing.*

He turned to his left and reached down for his book bag. He
unzipped the bag's main opening, reached in, and pulled out a
five-subject notebook.

There, he thought as he placed the notebook on the table
before him. *My notebook that has my novel outline.* Between
the coils of the notebook was a Pentel mechanical .7 lead pencil.
He grabbed the pencil in his right hand, flipped a few pages of
the notebook, and started skimming his outline:

Reporter –BDN

Cindy. Engagement ring.

Basic

Murdock – Pain is good. Pain is just weakness leaving the
body

He kept reading the entries on that particular notebook page, and he occasionally penciled in a new entry in his outline. Then, twenty minutes later, he closed his notebook and he resumed reading Truman Capote's *In Cold Blood*.

CHAPTER TWENTY-EIGHT

Mail Call started at 2000 hours and was over in its usual twenty minutes or so.

"Okay pukes, today was a fine Army day," said Drill Sergeant Murdock. He was sitting on a solid plastic red milk cart situated in the middle of the large dayroom. "We had a good Qualification Day, some good PT, and now we just finished with Mail Call. Phone privileges are till 2100 hours. Lights out at the normal 2200. Tomorrow we start our CTT Common Tasks Training." He quickly spat some tobacco juice into a plastic water bottle. "Good job, Charlie-4-10. Remember to stay focused and not let your guard down. Stay alert, stay alive. Y'all can use the phones. Remember—lights out at 2200."

Boudreau, like the other recruits, was wearing clean PT shorts and a PT shirt. As soon as he heard Murdock release the company, he—like many recruits—headed outside to use one of the pay phones.

Sure hope Cindy's at home tonight, he thought as he got in line behind one of the phone booths. He was third in line, then two other recruits got behind him.

Man, I haven't heard Cindy's voice in awhile. Hope I talk to her tonight. I also gotta call my folks and thank them for the letters they've been sending me.

Suddenly, Boudreau heard a voice behind him. "Hey J.B."

Boudreau turned to see that it was fellow-squad member Carey walking in his direction.

"J.B., somehow not one but two of your letters got tangled with mine," Carey said as he stood next to Boudreau. "That's why Drill Sergeant Murdock didn't call out your name during Mail Call—he didn't realize that two smaller letters were stuck to the big envelope I received."

"For real?" said Boudreau, excited.

"Absolutely," said Carey. "I didn't realize it until I went to open my big envelope. That's when I found your letters stuck to mine. Here you go." He handed Boudreau the two small letters.

"Hey thanks, Carey," Boudreau said, smiling. He grabbed the letters. "And congrats on qualifying this morning."

"Yeah, thanks. Can't believe I qualified," replied Carey. He turned around and started walking back toward the nearby barracks.

Boudreau looked at the first letter.

It's from Cindy. About time.

He immediately opened the letter.

"Hey dude, line's opening up. You're next," said the recruit standing directly behind Boudreau.

Boudreau looked ahead and noticed a recruit exiting the phone booth. He turned to the recruit who had just given him the heads up. "You guys go ahead," said Boudreau. He stepped to the side to let the other recruits advance. "I'm gonna read these letters first."

He removed Cindy's letter from its envelope and read it:

May 10, 1994

Jack,

I know this is my first letter to you since you left for your Army training, and I regret to inform you that it will be my last. Please don't take this the wrong way, Jack. I did get your phone messages, and I did plan on writing to you sooner, but the words—they just weren't coming to me—and as you know, good writing takes time. And though this isn't a well-written letter, it does express the main thing that I should have communicated to you for some time now.

Both of us are still young, Jack, and right now I just want to be free. Being free is not only fair to me, it's also fair to you. Please— and I really mean this— please don't think your enlistment in the Army had anything to do with this, because it just plain didn't. You know I support your decision to join the Army.

As I'm writing this letter to you, my short-term plans are in order. I've decided to continue my graduate studies in English but in Europe instead of here in Maine. I'll be traveling to England with Tom Lerner. Yes, the Tom Lerner who had an internship at the Bangor Daily News. *We leave in two days so by the time you read this we'll already be across the pond in Leeds, England. By the way, in case you're wondering, there's nothing between me and Tom—it's simply platonic, a friendship, that's all.*

I want to be free, Jack; I need to be free. I always wanted to study in Europe, and now I've got the chance.

I'll end by stating that you're a good guy and a good writer. I believe in you, Jack. I hope you'll achieve all that you want in life.

Take Care and Good Luck in the Army,

Cin

P.S. You're probably wondering about the apartment lease. Well, I've sublet our apartment to Lisa. Remember Lisa? She and Keith—Keith the assistant manager at the Dominoes you used to work at. Well, Lisa and Keith used to date, but they split up recently. Lisa said she'll rent the place for at least six months.

P.S.S. The Volvo is still making noise.

Man-oh-man, thought Boudreau. *Fuck.* His mind was racing. He knew it was bad with Cindy ... but still ... *it hurts.* He took a deep breath. He wasn't completely surprised, but, in the back of his mind, he had been hopeful. Hopeful that things would get better; that things would patch up; that Cindy would move back in with him once Basic Training was done; that they would be a couple again. Now this. The Jody Letter. The Dear John Letter.

Game over. *Christ.* He took another deep breath. *And now there's another rooster in the hen house. Frigg'in Tom Lerner. That fucking, pencil-dick, high-class piece of shit. Drives that shiny BMW.* Hell, the only reason he got that internship was 'cause of his dad's deep pockets and minority ownership in the Bangor Daily News. *Fuck man, simply platonic. A friendship. My ass it's simply platonic. Fuck.*

He shook his head in frustration.

And friggin' Lisa in the apartment. Can it get any worse for me, man? Jesus! Lisa can't rub two dimes together—how the hell will she pay the rent? And she better not touch my books, my cassettes, and my weight bench. Ah, man, and the phone. Crap— Lisa has all these friends and shit. She'll rack up huge phone bills. I wouldn't doubt that Cindy forgot to end our phone service. Lisa's probably using our phone account— or my phone account—now that Cindy fucking left me.

He folded the letter and placed it in its envelope. He slowly started walking toward the barracks.

He heard, "Hey guy, you sure you don't want to use the phone?" but he didn't respond. He just kept walking toward the barracks. His mind was spinning and emotions filled him: anger, frustration, and fear too, because the unknown is always unsettling.

No more engagement —now what? How will I tell my friends about this breakup? My parents—what will they think? How will Lisa of all people pay the rent?

And he also felt jealousy. *Tom Lerner. Fucking Tom Lerner. Cindy's in Europe with fucking Tom Lerner.*

He kept walking slowly. He tried to make sense of it all. Then, suddenly, he noticed he was holding another letter, the other letter Carey had given him along with Cindy's letter. He read the return address: Kaplan Jewelers, Brewer, Maine. *Hmmn?* He immediately tore open the envelope and read its contents. It was a statement. Purchase—diamond engagement ring. Minimum amount due: $89.00. Amount due by May 29th.

Sweet, he thought, shaking his head. *Jesus.*

CHAPTER TWENTY-NINE

While Boudreau and his C-4-10 comrades were midway through their eight-week Basic Training, Boros and his crew (Jackson, Jose, and Carlos) were busily occupied in the marijuana transport business. Their product came from Kentucky; their final markets came in the form of Missouri's two principal cities—St. Louis and Kansas City.

Boros coordinated everything. Jackson was in charge of security (this meant he drove the look-out security car), and Jose and Carlos took turns driving the cash crop in Jose's used but reliable souped-up Honda Civic.

Boros ran the operation like a tight ship—failure wasn't an option, defects weren't tolerated, and the rules of the game were followed precisely. One such rule Boros insisted on was what he called his "Nothing Flashy" rule.

"Here's what happened at Fort Campbell; true story guys," he once told his boys over beers and smokes at Leavenworth's hot spot, the 2010 Club.

"Military dude was working for a drug dealer, right? and making good bank with it—he was making good money. And what did this knucklehead military dude do? He screwed up royally by paying forty grand in cash for a brand new BMW Beemer with all the fixins."

"What's wrong with that?" asked a puzzled Jose who was nursing a Bud Light. "Car like that will bring some major pussy. Heck, I'd buy those wheels if I could."

"What's wrong with that picture?" retorted Boros, sarcastically. "Grow a fucking brain, Jose. Dude's a fucking PFC and pays cash for a car like that. See, the car dealers report shit like that. Low-paid PFC paying cash for expensive wheels raises flags and eyebrows, my boys. Dealer called the cops; cops started sniffing around; and the next thing you know the PFC's getting asked a lot of questions. He finally caves in and sings like a canary—tells the pigs he works for a drug dealer. Whole fucking operation gets compromised because the knucklehead bought an expensive Beemer, and he paid cash on top of that."

Boros took a sip from his Corona.

"Nothing flashy, boys. That's the rule. We save our dinero. We can buy some tunes here and there; take our chicks out to restaurants; and party at clubs and shit—but nothing flashy. Flashy attracts attention and the cops. Fancy clothes, jewelry, cars—the pigs look for that shit. They know a private first class is lucky to make twenty grand a year. How the fuck could a dude like that buy a brand new Beemer for forty grand cash."

"Roger, boss," said Jackson, nodding his head in approval. "Boss is right on, fellas. Let's keep everything on the low-down. We're low on the military totem pole—we ain't officers and shit. People know we don't rake in the big bucks."

"That's right. Keep things on the low-down," reiterated Boros. "Nothing flashy. Our ETSs are less than two years away. Once we leave the Army and report to Fort Living Room civilian life, then we can start living larger."

He touched beer bottles with each of his Boys.

"Cheers, gents."

"Cheers."

"Oh, and one more rule of the game."

"What's that, boss?" asked a curious Carlos.

"Another rule: no partaking of our product. No weed smoking, no snorting coke. I can't afford any of you failing one of those periodic Army urinalysis. I can't have any of you popping hot on a piss test."

CHAPTER THIRTY

Where weeks three and four of Boudreau's Basic Training were characterized by BRM training culminating with a Qualification Day, weeks five and six were characterized by CTT (Combat Task Testing) training ending in a CTT Test Day.

Boudreau enjoyed the grind of the daily CTT training:

What are your three general orders? What are the seven terrain features on a map? How do you do a functions check on the M16? What are the steps in setting up the claymore mine? How do you evaluate a casualty? Demonstrate the steps in administrating CPR? Don and clear your NBC mask in nine seconds.

Such were examples of the CTT skills Boudreau and the other C-4-10 recruits were learning every day—days that started with an early rising, then breakfast chow, then marching to a training site, then practicing the CTT skills with a battle buddy, then more CTT training, then daily PT sessions, then dinner chow, then Mail Call, then phone privileges, then polish boots and get BDU uniform ready for the next day. Lights out was always at 2200 sharp.

Boudreau enjoyed that daily routine and the CTT training, and his PT—*still working on my sit-ups because it's my worst event*— continued to be solid. The whole Cindy thing and its baggage aftermath— *she left me for Tom; Cindy kept the diamond ring that I'm still paying for; doubt if Lisa can pay the rent; is Lisa racking up humongous phone bills?; my Volvo*

115

is dying—all this troubled him, but he was slowly adjusting to *life after Cindy*. At times such baggage aftermath crept in his thoughts, but for the most part he was focused on the present and on doing well with the training at hand. And his attitude vis-à-vis Cindy was straightforward: *It's over. Finito. Closure. To the future. Move on. FIDO, man— fuck it, drive on.*

CHAPTER THIRTY-ONE

B oros's marijuana transport business was running steady and on track, but the same couldn't be said about his marijuana *growing* enterprise. He eventually scrapped the latter all together.

"You're making the right call, boss," said Jackson as he reassured Boros about dropping the pot growing. The two GI partners-in-crime were in Boros's barracks room at Fort Leavenworth. Both were smoking cigarettes and drinking beer.

"Growing weed's complicated, boss. It's high maintenance, man. Then you gotta worry 'bout weather, and you never know when some country redneck landowner dude discovers we planted some pot plants on his land patch. It's good we dumping the weed growing. We never did get a crop out."

"Yeah, Jackson, the weed growing has been nothing but headaches," Boros said. He took a sip from his Corona. "Plus we're probably gonna transport more and more pot 'cause L.D. wants to meet with me tonight. Said he's got an offer for us."

"That's cool, man," Jackson said. He was holding a bottle of Miller Genuine Draft in his right hand. "We's moved product for him before, right?"

"Yep, we sure have."

Five hours later, Boros met with L.D., Kansas City's second-largest drug dealer.

Chapter Thirty-Two

"MREs for lunch, pukes," said Drill Sergeant Murdock. The time was eleven thirty AM and Murdock was standing at the head of the company formation.

"I know many of y'all are almost done with your Common Task Testing and that's good, but we all need to break for lunch. Today pukes, we ain't getting a hot meal out here in the field—no hot meal from our trusted Gut Truck. It's MRE time. Yeah, some of you may not like these Meals Rejected by Ethiopians, but I'll tell y'all what—MREs will fill your fat candy asses up; plenty of good calories in them brown plastic bags. Fact is pukes, Meals Ready to Eat are good rations that will keep you going. Plus, when we do our FTX field training exercise next week, we'll always be eating MREs for lunch, so get used to them. Everybody tracking?"

"Hooah," replied the C-4-10 recruits.

Murdock quickly spat some tobacco juice on the ground, then said, "All righty then. Now like I said earlier, our CTT testing is going well. Many of you sorry asses will be done with CTT in a couple hours, but we ain't leaving this test site until everyone finishes. Remember—one team, one fight. Tracking Charlie-4-10?"

A loud "Hooah" from the recruits in formation.

"Also, I want to remind y'all that as of today we are three quarters done with Basic Training. I don't want any of y'all to put your guard down now. Stay focused, Charlie-4-10—keep your head in the game. Stay alert, stay alive. Tracking?"

The recruits came back with another loud, "Hooah."

"Good. We started with 120 of y'all, and now this company is down to one hundred fifteen, pukes. We've had a coupla Broke Dicks who had to be recycled, and we also had a few knuckleheads who couldn't hang and adapt to a military lifestyle. Those knuckleheads got chaptered out and sent back to Fort Living Room and civilian life, but overall, gang, I think y'all's a pretty good company."

"Hooah!" yelled the recruits in unison.

"Just don't let your guard down," Murdock reminded the recruits. "If you need to work on your PT, then put in some extra time on PT. Basically pukes, failing the APFT is the only damn thing that can prevent your ass from graduating from Basic Training. Everybody tracking?"

Another loud "Hooah" from the recruits.

"Good," said Murdock. "Now enjoy y'all's MREs. CTT testing resumes at 1300 hours sharp."

* * *

"What's your MRE, J.B.?" Bodette asked his battle buddy. The two were sitting at a wooden picnic table at the CTT test site. Also eating their MREs at the picnic table were Bodin, Brown, Carey, Carrington, and Cassell.

"Tuna casserole," replied Boudreau. "How about you?"

"Chicken with rice, which I hate. Wanna switch?"

"Sure."

Carrington, who was sitting directly across from Carey, suddenly chimed in with, "Heard you're a Jew, Carey. Is that so?" He had a cocky smirk on his face.

Carey didn't respond; he just kept eating.

"What, you won't talk to me, Carey? I'm a fellow Second Squader."

Still no response from Carey.

"What, I ain't good enough for you Jews, you 'Chosen People?'"

There was an awkward silence, then Carey reluctantly said, "Yes Carrington, I'm Jewish. What is it to you?"

"Nothing," Carrington said, smiling. "It's just that you Jews are the Christ Killers, man. What's up with that? Why don't you Jews believe in Jesus? Jesus himself was a Jew, yunno."

Carey resumed eating and ignored Carrington. No one else at the picnic table spoke.

"Well Carey, buddy," added Carrington. "I just hope you 'Chosen People' types wise up and find Jesus, our savior."

CHAPTER THIRTY-THREE

"**J**ust transport dope for me, B. Whaddaya say?"
Boros and L.D. were both in L.D.'s souped-up, green, 1989 Lincoln Town car parked just outside a dilapidated basketball court in one of Kansas City's rundown neighborhoods. It was around eight thirty at night.

"We've done a little bizzness before. My word is good—you know that," said the heavy-set L.D.

"That's true," said Boros. "That's true."

"And B, you know I always pay on time."

"That's true, too, L.D., I know that." Boros shifted in the front passenger seat. "Tell you what, L.D. Gimme just a day to think things over. Alls I need is a day."

"Sure thing, fair enough," said the 240-pound L.D. He was wearing his usual garb of loose-fitting clothes, Nike shoes, and a red Kansas City Chiefs cap. "'Course just remember this, B—you know what L.D. stands for right?"

Boros shook his head in disapproval. "Nah, bro, I'm clueless. What does L.D. stand for?"

"Stands for Lots Dope. That's me, B. I have a lot of the product. And there's another thing related to Lots Dope. It's another L.D. too. It's the L.D. that really counts, bro. Know what that L.D. is?"

"Nope," said Boros. "Educate me, my man."

"Stands for Lots Dough. Dope brings the dough, B—it's what pays the bills and then some. You think hard 'bout that offer I'm making you."

CHAPTER THIRTY-FOUR

"Ten privates. I need ten of you," said the NCO heading the NBC CTT test site. "I know there's probably twenty of you here, but I can only test ten at a time. Give me the first ten."

Boudreau, standing behind Bodin, was the tenth and final soldier accepted into the test group.

"Good afternoon, privates. I'm Staff Sergeant Riley, and this is the NBC test site. As you all know, NBC stands for nuclear, biological, and chemical. Right now I need you all to pass me your grade sheets."

The ten C-4-10 recruits forwarded their CTT paper grading sheets.

"Thank you," said Riley as he placed the sheets on a nearby picnic table. He was of medium height but extremely thin. His narrow nose helped support his thick-frame and thick-lens military-issued eyeglasses.

"We test four skills at this site," Riley continued. "I know you all have Pro Masks, and, as you can see, we have ten sets of MOPP gear here." He pointed to the chemical suits, rubber gloves, and rubber boots occupying grass space next to him. "Everything's large or extra large, so it'll fit every one of you."

Riley paused and proceeded to take a gulp of water from one of his nearby canteens.

"Now I know you guys have been training up on this stuff. Bottom line, gang, NBC is no doubt the toughest of all the CTT skills. I know it's not easy, but there's really no reason to blow this station if you've practiced properly. Hopefully, you guys have been practicing putting on your mask in nine seconds because that's the one thing that seems to trip up recruits at this station. So far I'd say three out of ten recruits don't make the time limit. Should this be you, just keep doing the remaining steps like putting on your different MOPP gear and doing the decontamination. I'll then retest you on donning and clearing your PRO Mask in nine seconds. Everyone tracking?"

"Hooah," replied the ten recruits.

"Okay. Now I want you guys to stand behind one of the MOPP suits and gear," Riley said. He pushed his BCGs up from the tip of his nose. "There should be two decon kits with each MOPP set."

Boudreau, like the other recruits, walked to one of the MOPP gear suits lying on the grass.

"Good, I see all ten of you are behind a set of MOPP gear. And I see that you all have your Kevlars on with your chinstraps buckled. Everybody got their Pro Mask in their case I hope?"

Riley paused for just a couple of seconds.

"How about giving me a north-south on that one. Masks in case?"

All the recruits nodded in approval.

"Okay, lemme get my stopwatch out," said Riley. "Oh, and by the way, when you guys remove your Kevlars, be sure to place your Kevlar between your knees. I'm gonna gig you if you don't do that."

Sweet, thought Boudreau. *Another thing to worry about. This task is already challenging as it is.*

"All right now," Riley said. "Here we go." He was now holding a black stopwatch in his right hand. "Ready ... and ...gas!"

Each recruit immediately closed his eyes, stopped breathing, unbuckled his Kevlar chin strap, placed his Kevlar helmet between his knees, and unvelcroed his Pro Mask carrying case, which was strapped to either his left or right hip.

Just as I practiced, thought Boudreau as he hurriedly placed his Pro mask over his head and face. He made a conscious effort to keep squeezing his knees together to ensure his Kevlar wouldn't hit the ground, and he also closed his mask carrying case by re-velcroing the case's cover. He pulled on his mask's rear adjustment straps, then he exhaled from the mouthpiece inside his mask, and then he placed his left hand on the Pro mask canister and his right hand on the exterior mouthpiece intake valve. He quickly sucked in some air which made him immediately feel his rubber facemask because the outward rim of the facemask collapsed around his cheeks and forehead. He flipped the thin green Pro mask protective hood over his head, neck, and the top of his shoulders all in one motion, then he yelled, "Gas! Gas! Gas!" and gave the gas signal—outstretched arms parallel to ground, touch the top of your shoulders.

"Time!" yelled Riley as he pressed the stop button on his stopwatch.

Whew, thought Boudreau. *Made the time limit, and my mask ain't fogged up. I think I got a good seal.*

"All right, let's see what we have," Riley said as he was about to grade the ten recruits.

"Two of you are still ate up and messing around with your masks. One of you didn't place the Kevlar between his knees. And I see that two of you forgot to snap shut your mask cases. As I walk around to check your seal, I'll tell you if you're a first-time GO or a NO GO at this station."

Boudreau crossed his fingers for good luck. *I think I did everything right. Did I close my mask carrying case? I know I've got a pretty good mask seal.* He started to doubt himself. Suddenly, he saw Riley walking in his direction.

"Breathe out, private," Riley ordered Boudreau. Boudreau breathed out. "Now suck in," Riley said as his hands covered Boudreau's exterior mask canister. "Good—you're a GO at this station, private. Put your K-pot on your head and proceed with the rest of your MOPP levels."

CHAPTER THIRTY-FIVE

"**O**kay, sounds like a plan, L.D."
Boros and L.D. were in a Kansas City bar discussing L.D.'s recent offer over drinks.

"You pay gas and other expenses?" asked Boros, his face close to L.D.'s because the music—MC Hammer's latest hit—was pretty loud.

"Nah, bro," said L.D. He rubbed his goatee with his fingers. "See, I don't work like that, B. I know what each shipment is worth on the street. That's why I give you a cut of the action. Fifteen percent."

"And what if my Boys get pulled over by the pigs?" asked Boros as he took a sip from his Corona.

"Now that shit flies," said L.D., nursing a rum and coke. "Those hassles are legit, and I'll cover them. Promise. See, I've got this fine-ass lawyer on retainer. Tall, good-looking Black dude who can talk his way out of any storm. Judges love him, and juries—especially Black jurors—love him even more. He ain't cheap, but he's gotten me out of some jams. Well worth the price." L.D. paused, then he said, "This sharp lawyer dude once told me most of his clients are Black, but he likes working for a white guy like me 'cause in the end, it's all about the green. Money, B. If the price is right, that fine-ass Black lawyer of mine will come through."

L.D. turned to a waitress and yelled, "Another rum and coke, honey."

He turned back to Boros and said, "I promise you, B, your dudes get pulled over, just tell them to keep their mouths shut, and I'll send my sharp lawyer over. 'Course there's one rule we bettah get straight, though."

"What's that?" asked an attentive Boros.

"My name never gets mentioned. Never."

"That's cool," said Boros. He took a quick sip from his beer. "I'm cool with that. And you promise me a shipment every weekend?"

"That's right," said L.D. "Every weekend. Delivery mostly here to KCMO, but sometimes to St. Louis, sometimes Omaha, and sometimes Denver. The bread and butter though is right here in KC."

"And you pay when?"

L.D. shifted in his chair. "Just like we've done before with those smaller loads. We negotiate on price beforehand so there ain't no surprises. Fifteen percent cut. Cash. I'll probably end up paying you by mid-week."

"What about pagers and cell phones? Who pays for those?"

"That's on you, B," said L.D. "But if you're having a hard time paying for the equipment and shit, then I can advance you some money. Same thing for gas—I can front you gas money and we deduct that from the total."

The two talked things over some more—details like driving routes, possible pick up and drop off times, and where they'd meet for payment. Boros liked everything he heard, and he was leaning toward accepting L.D.'s offer, but he had one more question. He took a sip from his Corona, and then he looked directly at the heavyset L.D.

"Bottom line, L.D.—can I trust you, man?"

L.D. leaned back in his sofa chair, and just as he was about to answer, the waitress arrived with his drink. "Thanks, honey." He handed her a ten dollar bill.

"B, it's like in the movie *Scarface*." He placed his drink on the glass table.

"Say again?" asked a confused Boros.

"*Scarface*. The movie. Al Pacino plays this tough cookie."
Boros still had no clue.

"Anyway B, in the movie *Scarface*, the Colombians ask Tony—that's the character played by Pacino—if they can trust him, and Tony tells 'em exactly what I'm about to tell you."

"What's that, L.D.? Whaddaya gonna tell me? Give it to me."

"Yeah you can trust me, B, 'cause like Pacino said in that movie: 'All I've got are my balls and my word, and I don't break either one.'"

CHAPTER THIRTY-SIX

"**O**kay pukes, CTT is done with," Drill Sergeant Murdock told the company of recruits in front of him.

It was a hot and humid late afternoon, and Charlie-4-10 had formed up outside the barracks.

"Overall, we had a good day of testing. Some of y'all had some NO GOs, but you properly adjusted fire, corrected those malfunctions, and retested. Good job, Charlie-4-10."

"Hooah," replied the three-platoon strong company.

"Tomorrow, we start our four-day FTX. Then we'll do our final PT test, and after that it's clean up the barracks for a final inspection. And yes, y'all will be wearing your Class A uniform for the inspection."

Murdock scanned the formation. He had his thick forearms crossed against his chest. He spat some tobacco juice on the grass next to him.

"And, after the FTX, it's y'all's graduation. Most of y'all will then fly outta here or bus outta here to y'all's AIT schools, but for you high-speed combat engineers, y'all's AIT is right here at lovely Fort Lost In The Woods."

He again spat tobacco chew juice on the grass.

"Okay, two more things to put out. One—and I do this with every Basic Training class— I'm officially issuing this fine company of pukes a challenge. That's right Charlie-4-10, I've got a challenge for y'all. Here it is: if y'all pass the final barracks inspection, then I promise to wear a pink ballerina suit to y'all's graduation."

Chuckles and laughs and some "hooahs" could be heard from the recruits. Murdock smiled.

"I'm serious Charlie-4-10. Scout's honor. If y'all pass my final inspection, then I'll wear a pink ballerina suit to y'all's graduation."

He briefly looked down at the ground, smiling.

"Now I must warn y'all that no Basic Training company has ever passed my final inspection, but don't let this discourage y'all. You never know, you pukes might be the first to get a GO on this final inspection. I warn y'all in advance—my standards are tough. Just clean them barracks real good. Attention to detail, pukes—attention to detail is the key. Clean and polish and mop and polish some more. Who knows? it can be done."

The recruits sounded off with a loud "Hooah."

"Heh, y'all, seeing me in a pink ballerina suit should be extra motivation for y'all to clean the barracks real good now. Is that right Charlie-4-10?"

"Hooah," yelled the recruits.

"Good," said Murdock. "So that's the barrack inspection challenge. What else? Oh yeah, here's the second thing—the joke of the day."

Murdock pointed to a recruit out of Second Platoon who was standing in front of him.

"Private, gimme your M16. Come on up here and gimme your M16."

The recruit took about five paces forward and handed Murdock his M16 weapon. Boudreau, standing at the position of at-ease in First Platoon, didn't recognize the Second Platoon recruit.

"Here's the joke of the day, Charlie-4-10," Murdock said smiling.

He said, "This is a weapon" as he pointed to the M16 the recruit had just handed him, "and this is my gun"—he pointed at his crouch.

"I use this for killing"—he was pointing at the M16 again.

Then he pointed at his crouch and said, "I use this for fun."

CHAPTER THIRTY-SEVEN

The arrangement for Boros and his Boys to be the sole transporters of drugs for L.D. was agreed upon to the beneficial and mutual satisfaction of both parties: L.D. was pleased he had reliable transportation for his product, and Boros was happily receiving a steady stream of cash for providing that transportation.

Boros and his Boys worked nearly every weekend in this drug transport business. They'd leave in two cars on Friday nights and pick up the drugs by Saturday morning in far-away Kentucky. Then it was the long drive back to St. Louis or Kansas City for the drop off. Boros and his Boys were always back in the Fort Leavenworth barracks by late Sunday night, and they always got paid by L.D. by Wednesday at the latest.

Sure, there was the Army rule requiring a mileage pass for any soldier wishing to travel more than one hundred miles from the military installation, but how could a company commander enforce such a rule? Boros and his Boys ignored that Army rule and the paperwork, time-consuming bureaucracy that came with it. Besides, they worked virtually every weekend. Asking for a mileage pass so frequently would definitely raise some eyebrows from the military brass.

CHAPTER THIRTY-EIGHT

"Yunno, this was fun in the beginning, but after awhile it gets boring."

"Roger that, battle buddy," Bodette told Boudreau. "You know the deal, Jack. There's a lot of hurry up and wait in the Army."

The two battle buddies were lying behind thick brush off a narrow trail about a half-mile from the FTX base camp. Their bellies were to the ground, and their faces were camouflaged with green, black, and gray Army camouflage paint. Boudreau, the appointed squad leader for the OPFOR (opposition forces) ambush site, was on the lookout for the squad of recruits who were slated to come up the trail. Bodette, lying within arm's reach of Boudreau, was the OPFOR radioman. Surrounding them in from all directions were thick woods.

"We've been here what? close to two hours, Jim? No sign of the enemy, man."

"I know it, I know it, J.B.," said Bodette as he readjusted his MILES gear. "Our engagements went well this morning. We kicked ass, man. And now Base Camp assures me Alpha-3-4 left about an hour ago."

"So they should be in sight by now, Jim," Boudreau said. He paused for a second. "Think they went off the trail? It's possible, you know."

"Doubt it, bud. Cassell's leading that squad, and he's pretty squared away. He's probably extra careful. Plus we need to be on the lookout for any flank moves. Trail's the easiest way for them to get to that small hut, but they could swing around the trail to avoid us high-speed OPFOR Opposition Forces."

There was a short pause, then Boudreau said, "Jim, call in another radio check just to make sure our commos are good."

"Roger that," replied Bodette as his right thumb pressed on the radio mike. "Base Camp, Base Camp, this is OPFOR-One. Radio check—over."

"Roger OPFOR-One. This is Base Camp. You're coming in five over five. Over."

"Base Camp, Base Camp, this is OPFOR-One. Roger, that's a good copy. OPFOR-One out." He released the mike button. "Radio's fine, Jack."

"Good," said Boudreau. "Everything fine behind me?"

Bodette turned around, scanned the terrain, and said, "Roger, Jack. Carey, Brown, Bodin— they're all in position with good concealment. No way Cassell's squad can see us. Unless of course they're making some flanking movement."

Seconds passed. No sound could be heard in the thick woods. Boudreau looked at his black Timex watch.

Fifteen hundred hours, he thought to himself. *Where is Cassell's squad?*

More quiet time. No sign of the squad they're supposed to engage.

"Well Jim, seeing that the enemy ain't in sight, lemme ask you battle buddy, what's been the best part of this Basic Training thing?"

"Jeez, let me see," said Bodette. He spoke quietly for only Boudreau to hear. "Uh, I'd have to say throwing those two live grenades shortly after Q-day. That was fun—learning about the tripod grip, pull the pin, throw, and boom! I actually felt the ground shake from underneath me in that grenade pit, man. That was cool. Everything else about Basic sucks, especially now that I've got a bit of poison ivy on my legs and butt." He paused for a sec. "How 'bout you, Jack? What's been your favorite? Y'all probably say PT. You know I'm rooting for ya to win the PT Award."

"Don't root too hard," Boudreau said as he kept scanning the area for Cassell's squad. "Moose from Third Platoon pretty much has it in the bag. Brother's built like a rock. Maxes his push-ups and sit-ups every time. Only slight weakness of his is his run time, but he's been doing some extra running with Drill Sergeant Carter. Moose maxed his run on our last diagnostic PT test. He's got it in the bag."

"What about the Leadership Award. You're probably in the running for that."

"Nah," Boudreau said, still scanning the terrain. "Baker's got that wrapped up in my opinion. He shot expert on Q-day, and his uniform and boots are spotless. He's done everything here perfectly. He's having a great Basic Training in my opinion."

"Yeah he is. Baker's a pretty sharp dude," said Bodette as he scratched his right thigh from the itchy poison ivy. "But I still think you're in the running. Anyway, what will it be, Jack? What's been your favorite thing about this Basic Training thing?

Boudreau thought for a moment while still looking out for Cassell's squad. "Well, I too enjoyed throwing the two live grenades, but if I had to pick one thing it'd be road marches."

"Road marches," Bodette said, shaking his head. "Jeez Jack. You're probably the only dude who would say that. Road marches." He shook his head again. "Man, those mother-fuckers have given me the worst blisters. I keep having to put on that moleskin stuff over my blisters just so I'm half-way comfortable when walking. Road marches—dude you're sick. And that reminds me—we've got that twenty-mile road march tonight as we head back to the barracks. What time does that sucker kick off again?"

"Oh one hundred hours, buddy," responded Boudreau.

He moved his legs to get more comfortable on the ground.

"Road march twenty miles back to the barracks. Sleep some, then clean the barracks for close to two days for that final inspection. Then it's a final PT test, turn in equipment, then the graduation. We're almost outta here, buddy."

"You better believe it, Jack. But I'm still curious, man—why road marches? Why's that your favorite part about Basic?"

Boudreau thought for a moment. "You know what it is, Jim? It's the peacefulness of it. When I'm road marching, I don't have to think about what's next. I don't have to do anything except put one foot in front of the other."

"What's so great about that?" asked Bodette as he resituated his radio antenna behind a nearby tree.

"Well, it allows me to think about stuff I want to think about. Like my upcoming AIT or books I want to read or books I want to write or what my favorite movies are—things like that. Sometimes when we're road marching, I think about stuff that worries me too though—upcoming bills, my apartment back in Maine, my old car. I also think about Cindy here and there, but less and less."

"Good," said Bodette. "You did the right thing by ditching the bitch."

"Well Jim, buddy, to be fair about it, she actually left me. I didn't leave her—she ditched me."

"Same difference, Jack," said Bodette matter-of-factly. "She left you means it wouldn't of lasted anyway. She wasn't loyal to you, my friend. There's plenty of better girls out there for you."

"Well thanks for the word of confidence, Jim. Appreciate that. I'll move on. I'll start dating again once things settle down."

There was silence for a few seconds, then Bodette said, "So, peaceful thinking huh? Yeah, I guess you can do that while road marching. Lately for me, my thoughts have been about Korea. I know that's where I'm heading after my AIT here at Fort Lost in the Woods. DMZ Korea. Probably get myself killed there, man. Go figure."

"Nah, bud, you'll be okay," Boudreau said. His tone was reassuring. "North Koreans are a strange bunch, but they won't try anything funny. You'll be okay there."

"Sure hope so, man. Damn my legs itch." He scratched his right thigh again.

A few silent seconds passed.

"So, writer, huh? An interest in writing books," Bodette said, curious. "I know you're the Army reporter dude. Who are your favorite writers, Jack?"

"Well, my favorite writer is Michael Crichton. I really like his stuff. John Grisham is probably my second favorite. Tom Clancy's is another good one. John Irving. Tom Wolfe. Stephen King from my home state of Maine. There's so many. Probably the best writer I ever read is Truman Capote. He wrote this great book entitled *In Cold Blood*. I've read it once, but I'd like to read it again. Have you heard of it, Jim? Have you heard of *In Cold Blood*."

"Can't say that I have," said Bodette. "I don't recognize any of those names you've mentioned except Stephen King and John Grisham. I guess I don't read much." He then quickly changed the subject by asking, "What about movies, Jack? What's your favorite movie? Mine's *Star Wars*."

"For me, I'd have to say *A Few Good Men*. Great flick. It's written by Aaron Sorkin. He's another great writer."

"I think I saw that movie," said Bodette as he looked out for Cassell's squad. "Tom Cruise right? Demi Moore's also in it."

"That's right," said Boudreau. "Jack Nicholson too. He plays the Marine Colonel. Great flick, man. Awesome dialogue. Sorkin's such a great writer."

"Yeah, I liked the movie too. Plus Demi Moore's such a hotty."

"Yep, sure is," said Boudreau. "I like that scene where the other lawyer asks her, 'Why do you like them so much?' You know, he's asking her why she likes the Marines so much, and she tells him, 'Because they stand on a wall, and they say nothing's gonna harm you. Not tonight. Not on my watch.' That's a great scene, man. I figure that—"

"J.B. we got action," Bodette said, cutting him off. "My two o'clock position. 'Bout a hundred meters."

Boudreau immediately looked at that vicinity. "Roger, I have eyes on. Give the thumbs up to Carey, Brown, and Bodin. Time to play soldier, boys. Fire blanks till you hear the beep sound of the enemy's MILES gear."

CHAPTER THIRTY-NINE

A fter a steady month of the Kentucky-to-drug-drop-off site travels, Boros mustered the courage to ask L.D. for cell phones, pagers, and 9mm handguns.

"Our loads are getting bigger, L.D. We're pushing a lot of product for you, bro," Boros reminded L.D. one Thursday night at Kansas City's Chica Club. "We need good communications, and you never know when things can go wrong. Guns, phones, and pagers, L.D. We need them. I know you told me when we made this deal that that shit was on me, but I'm asking you to reconsider, bud."

L.D. sipped some rum and coke from his glass. He looked deep in thought, his face frowning. He then nodded his head.

"Well I guess I can buy that shit 'cause your boys have been doing good work for me."

"Thanks, bro," said Boros. "It's cool, man. We like your business, L.D."

"Y'all have the cell phones and pages by early next week."

"Nice, L.D. We appreciate that, my man."

L.D. shifted in his chair. "Four handguns, huh? That'll take me longer, but y'all get them soon enough."

CHAPTER FORTY

Barracks Inspection Day. All C-4-10 recruits had spent the last two days cleaning and scrubbing the barracks, and not a detail had gone unnoticed—bunks were made to perfection, floors were buffed so they shone with reflections, and all brass hardware items had received healthy coats of Brasso and elbow-grease scrubbing.

"Mornin' pukes," Drill Sergeant Murdock said loudly as soon as he entered the barracks.

Each recruit was attired in his Class A uniform and was standing at the position of attention next to his bunk. Murdock, too, was in his Class A uniform. He was also carrying an empty plastic water bottle that served as a spitoon.

Murdock took a sharp left and entered the barrack's first bay area, the bay area occupied by Boudreau and his fellow squad members.

"Good mornin y'all," Murdock said as soon as he entered the room. "Y'all know the deal. Pass this inspection and I'll wear some flimsy ballerina outfit at y'all's graduation."

He started walking around the room. "Good morning, PFC Bodette."

"Good morning, drill sergeant," said an erect Bodette.

"And good mornin', Private Carrington."

"Good morning, drill sergeant," said a stoic Carrington.

Murdock stood still and looked around the room. "Y'all are doing well as a squad," he said. "Hey, just three more days and a wake up, right?"

"Hooah," replied the squad members.

"Good job," said Murdock as he spat some tobacco juice into the empty plastic water bottle. "I've seen all I wanna see here. Why don't you squared-away recruits follow me to the nearest latrine."

Murdock turned on his heal and exited the bay room. The eight recruits followed in tow.

"Okay pukes, gather 'round me," Murdock said as soon as he entered the nearest barracks latrine. He placed his tobacco spit bottle on the flat portion of a nearby sink, and then he removed his Class A coat and "here you go Private Carey. Why don't you hold on to my Class A coat while I check something out."

"Roger, drill sergeant," answered Carey, the recruit nearest Murdock.

Murdock then quickly removed his black tie and light-green, long-sleeve Class A shirt. He handed those to Carey as well.

Murdock, now just wearing his white T-shirt and Class A pants, opened the nearest toilet stall. He walked up to the toilet bowl and took a knee. "Gather round boys, and check out what I'm 'bout to do."

Boy, Boudreau thought as he and the others gathered around the stall. *There must be a catch to this. Something's up.*

Murdock was now bent down and holding the toilet rim with his left hand. His right arm was totally immersed inside the toilet bowl. By the look of Murdock's squinting eyes and contorted face, Boudreau could tell Murdock was searching for something.

"There," said Murdock. He was smiling now. "I think I found what I expected."

He stood up. Something was in his right hand, but Boudreau couldn't make it out.

Murdock walked to the nearest bathroom mirror, a bathroom mirror above a thick white porcelain sink.

"What I've got here pukes is shit. Ka-ka. Dung. Crapola, pukes. I've got crap in my right hand," said a smiling Murdock as he faced the squad. "Y'all did an A-One job cleaning and polishing and mopping. Y'all did a decent job cleaning the toilets too, but you didn't go deep enough down there, which is why I've got shit in my right hand." He turned, faced the mirror, and scribbled NG/BL with the feces in his right hand.

"NG/BL, pukes. Stands for NO GO/Bo-low. Y'all failed this inspection. Good try though."

The recruits stood still, stunned. Dead silence permeated the room. Murdock, sporting a big smile, washed and rinsed his hands and dried them off by using a nearby hot air hand blower.

"Heh, any of y'all fine recruits bowl any? Do I have any bowlers here?" asked Murdock as he walked back to the sink. He extended his right arm toward Carey who handed him his Class A coat, shirt, and tie.

"Any bowlers here?"

Silence for maybe five seconds, then Carrington, who was standing next to Carey, said, "I am, drill sergeant. I bowl a lot actually."

"Is that so?" Murdock said, smiling again.

"Roger that, drill sergeant," said Carrington, his tone a confident one. "In fact, drill sergeant, I've got a 210 bowling average. Someday I hope to qualify for the PBA tour."

"Well, heh now," Murdock said loudly, "we've got ourselves a pro here."

Carrington smiled.

"Well since you're such a great bowler, Carrington, why don't you clean the toilet bowls in this here latrine. We need a fine bowler like you to get all the shit outta these toilet bowls."

Carrington's face immediately turned beet red. Everyone was standing still and silent, then Murdock suddenly burst out laughing, which brought laughs from everyone except Carrington.

"You're the right man for that shitty detail," Murdock said, holding back more laughs.

Some of the squad members started laughing out loud.

Carrington, trying to gain his composure, searched for some rebuttal. He looked at Carey.

"Stop laughing, Carey," he said. "Stop laughing, you smartass."

Carey, his shoulders shrugging from trying to hold back laughs, looked liked he had something to say. He swallowed hard, then he looked directly at Carrington and said:

"Better to be a smartass than a dumbass."

CHAPTER FORTY-ONE

B oudreau was reading Capote's *In Cold Blood.*
Man, what a writer Capote was, he thought as he finished reading a paragraph. *Awesome writer. What a talent. He's an inspiration.* He looked at his watch.

Gosh, so much has happened since last weekend. I hope Carlos's a straight-shooter. I think so; I think he'll tell me what I need to know.

Boudreau's thoughts shifted; he started thinking about that novel of his. He opened his notebook and picked up the nearby mechanical pencil. He started reading some of the entries:

Cindy—break up. Tom Lerner—another rooster in the hen house. Ouch!

Q-day. Shot sharpshooter
Threw two live grenades
Carey is Jewish
Carrington—anti-Semitic
CTT training—all first-time GOs
Barracks Inspection—funny. Murdock's inspection unpassable

Then a thought hit him. He penciled in: *Bodette— BB. His AIT's at Fort Lost in the Woods. He's worried about Korea. Said* Star Wars *was his favorite flick.* He also wrote: *Capote was a great writer; know what you write; write what you know.*

He then looked up at one of the nearby walls of the bookstore.

Orwell, Nabokov, Whitman, Elliot, Steinbeck, Faulkner.

He thought: *Someday it will be Grisham and King and Clancy and Crichton too. And the great Capote belongs on these walls as well. Tom Wolfe, John Irving, Saul Bellow, and Norman Mailer, too.*

CHAPTER FORTY-TWO

Basic Training Graduation Day. The entire graduation ceremony—national anthem, handing out certificates, guest speaker (a retired lieutenant colonel filled that role), presentation of awards, playing of the Army song—took all of thirty minutes. The ceremony occurred inside an old movie theater not too far from the C-4-10 barracks. Now, the company of recent graduates was in formation in front of the barracks. Boudreau, like the other 113 graduates, was wearing his Class A uniform. It was a hot and muggy mid-June late morning. Boudreau was sweating, and the glare from the sun made his eyes squint.

"Congrats pukes. You bunch of fucks made it," said Murdock from the head of the formation. He too was in his Class A uniform.

"I'm proud of y'all, and I can honestly say y'all been my best Basic Training company in my eighteen months as a drill sergeant."

"Hooah," replied the newly-graduated recruits.

Murdock continued. "A few of y'all won awards today, and I congratulate the awardees, but the bottom line is y'all performed well as a company."

Another loud "Hooah." Boudreau, standing at the position of parade-rest from Second Squad, First Platoon, had not won any awards. In fact, as he had predicted, Moose did win the top PT Award while Baker took down the Top Dawg Award, the award given to the overall best recruit of the company. The Leadership Award went to Private Mathison, a Second Platoon member.

"We started this Basic Training eight weeks ago," Murdock said in a loud and commanding voice. "And on Day One I asked y'all to show me—a native Missourian—I asked y'all to show me something, to show me what you guys were made of. Well y'all did show me something. Y'all showed me you can work as a team, that y'all could work as a company."

"Hooah," replied the C-4-10 recruits.

"Now y'all will leave this place for your upcoming AITs, your advanced individual training. Some of y'all will fly to y'all's AIT site, some of y'all will be on a Greyhound Bus shortly and get bused to your AIT site, and some of y'all will stay put right here at lovely Fort Lost In The Woods to do your AIT here. Wherever y'all end up, good luck, and thanks for enlisting in the Army."

Another loud "Hooah" from the new graduates.

"The time is now close to 1000 hours," continued Murdock. "Be sure to say your goodbyes to y'all's battle buddies and your loved ones who attended this morning's graduation, and then be sure to pick up y'all's belongings and duffle bags in the barracks. And for those of y'all getting on a Greyhound bus, those buses will be here in around thirty mikes. Everyone tracking?"

"Hooah," replied the graduates.

"Okay Charlie-4-10, it's time to say goodbye. How 'bout saying y'all's company motto one last time. Company—attention!"

The graduates snapped to the position of attention and recited their motto:

The Law.
This is the house of pain.
Are we not men?
No, we are not men, we are beasts.
And Charlie Company has made us beasts.
We will not walk.
We will not talk.
We will not gather in the night.
We are highly trained to kill.

Our last resort is cold steel.

Jab! between the second and third rib.

Twist!

Aaaaaaaaahhhh Hooah!

"Excellent," said Murdock. "God speed to everyone of y'all. Remember: stay alert, stay alive. Dismissed!"

The formation broke up. Boudreau, hot and sweaty, proceeded to shake hands with every First Platoon, Second Squad member. Like about half of the recruits, he didn't have any visitors to his graduation on account of the long distance from his home state.

"Good luck to you, Jim," he said as he shook hands with his battle buddy. Bodette was the last person to shake hands with Boudreau. "And good luck here with your AIT and then Korea."

"Thanks, Jack," said a perspiring Bodette. "And same to you—good luck. Maybe you'll write that best-selling book someday and I'll hear all about it."

"Thanks, man," said Boudreau, then he started heading toward the barracks.

"Oh and Jack," he heard Bodette say. He turned to face him. Bodette was giving him the thumbs up. "Jack, just remember: stay alert, stay alive."

"Roger that, battle buddy." He saluted Jim.

* * *

Boudreau entered the barracks and immediately went into the bay room where his bunk was located. On his bunk were his two large Army duffle bags. Everything he came to Basic Training with was packed in those duffle bags.

I'm gonna need some reading material for that upcoming long-ass bus ride, he told himself as he unlocked and opened up one of the duffle bags. *Ah here, that should do it.* He pulled out two books —a Crichton paperback, *Jurassic Park*, and Capote's *In Cold Blood*.

Boudreau closed the duffle bag, relocked it, and strapped it over his right shoulder and upper back; he carried the other duffle bag by holding the bag's handle strap in his right hand; he carried the two books in his left hand.

He exited the bay room, veered right, and headed down the hallway.

"Hey Jack, good luck to you," he heard. It was Private Richardson, a Second Platoon recruit who had served on KP duty (kitchen police) with Boudreau back during the second week of Basic.

"Thanks Joe. Same to you, bud," replied Boudreau. He stopped to shake hands with Richardson. "Are you staying here or heading off elsewhere for your AIT?"

"Staying put, man. MOS is combat engineer. Drills told us we're all heading to Korea after our AIT. How 'bout you, Jack? Journalist, right? Where's your AIT again?"

"Indianapolis. Fort Benjamin Harrison. Greyhound bus leaves in twenty mikes or so. I think it's like a seven-hour bus ride."

"Shit's cool, man," said the short and slim Richardson. Then he added, "Hey Jack. Check out what Drill Sergeant Murdock posted on the training board next to the Wuss Sheet." Richardson pointed. "I just read it."

Boudreau took three steps forward and read the thumb-tacked typed letter on the announcement cork board.

FROM: Drill Sergeant Murphy
TO: Charlie-4-10 Pukes
SUBJECT: Great words spoken by one of our greatest Presidents, Theodore Roosevelt. (Also, pay attention to the P.S. and P.S.S. lines).
I choose not to be a common man.
It's my right to be uncommon if I can.
I'll seek opportunity, not security.
I do not wish to be a kept citizen, humbled and dulled by having the state look after me.

I want to take the calculated risk, to dream and to build, to fail and to succeed. I'll refuse to live from hand to mouth.

I prefer the challenges of life to the guaranteed existence, the thrill of fulfillment to the calm state of Utopia.

I will never cower before any master, nor bend to any threat.

It is my heritage to stand erect, proud and unafraid, to think and act for myself and face the world boldly and say,

THIS I HAVE DONE.

T.R.

P.S. Annoy a liberal—work hard and smile.

P.S.S. Remember: stay alert, stay alive.

Drill Sergeant Murdock

Ten minutes after reading that passage, Boudreau was on a Greyhound bus bound for Indianapolis.

"A conflagration took place. No, we don't write like that. Write a fire broke out... It does you no good to write conflagration when you mean a fire."

Quote from Air Force Tech Sergeant Mike McNeil
to his new DINFOS journalism students.
June, 1994
Fort Benjamin Harrison, Indiana

CHAPTER FORTY-THREE

"**F**ort Benjamin Harrison," Boudreau told the taxi driver. The cab had just pulled into Indianapolis's main Greyhound Bus terminal, and Boudreau had just placed his two duffle bags in the back seat. He opened the front passenger door and got into the cab.

"No need to tell me where you're heading, stud," replied the taxi driver. "I see you're in uniform; you're heading to Fort Ben."

The cab sped away, and in less than two minutes Boudreau was able to see the city's skyline.

Man, what a view, he thought, marveling at the tall buildings. *I've been in the deep Missouri woods for the past two months. It's good to be back with civilization.*

"What you in for stud?" asked the cab driver as he was about to merge onto the highway. He was big—6-4, 250-pound big—mid-thirtyish age-wise, and wearing blue jeans and a Pacers T-shirt. A Pacers cap was affixed atop his bushy brown hair.

"What's your AIT about, stud?"

"46 Quebec," said Boudreau, still admiring the skyline. "I'll be training as an Army journalist."

"That's cool, man, cool shit. We don't get too many of those," said the taxi driver. He spoke fast and in a deep voice.

"We get a lot of postal MOSs and also finance, but we don't get too many journalists."

The cab sped onto the highway. Boudreau had his passenger window half-open. The blowing warm humid air felt good on him.

"Mind if I smoke, stud?" asked the driver earnestly. "I'll leave a crack in my window— promise."

"Sure, no problem," answered Boudreau even though he didn't like the smell of cigarette smoke.

The driver pulled out a cigarette from the pack lying next to the gear shift box. "Say, I see you're an E-4 Specialist, stud," he said as he reached for a lighter under the radio. He lit the cigarette and took a puff

Got college or what? E-4 straight outta Basic is kinda rare."

"Yessir, I've got a college degree," said Boudreau. He was still looking at the buildings.

"Shit man, I was in the Army for three-and-a-half years," said the driver, his cigarette now between his right index and middle fingers.

"It took me that long to make the rank of specialist."

Boudreau, saying nothing, kept soaking in the city landscape.

"Yeah, man, for me, the Army wasn't all that bad, but I didn't want to do it as a career. So here I am, a cab driver during the day and a bouncer at a titty bar at night. You're my last drive for tonight.

Boudreau, sensing he should say something, replied, "That's interesting."

"Name's Mike by the way," said the driver. He extended his right hand toward Boudreau.

"Jack Boudreau."

They shook hands.

"Boudreau, huh? That's French, right? You must be Cajun or from New England."

"That's right, sir," said Boudreau. "I'm from Maine."

The driver took another puff from his cigarette, then he exhaled in the direction of his half-opened window.

"Hell stud, I can tell you're straight from Basic—calling me 'sir' and shit. Call me Mike, man."

"Yessir," said Boudreau, but he immediately caught himself. "Uh, sure Mike."

"Yeah, man, we cab drivers like you military guys. As soon as you guys get privileges during AIT, then some of you frequent Indy's titty bars, and that's good for our business. Plus, this taxi ride is free to you by the way. We're paid by the military base for transporting you to or from the airport or the bus station. I'll just need you to sign a paper."

"Sure thing," said Boudreau. He was still absorbing the city landscape.

"Shit, Frenchy, I just drove to Fort Ben two days ago. I picked up some nigger soldier at the bus station right, and I brought him to the base. Stupid me, I started talking guns and rap music and chicks with the brother, right. I guess I got all excited 'cause I had the rap station on, and the next thing I know, I was doing forty-five in a thirty. Guess what happened, Frenchy?"

"Uh, not sure, Mike," Boudreau said in an uninterested way. "What happened?"

"I got pulled over by an MP, that's what happened, but let me tell you, she was this hotty man, real fine looking. Short little Filipino MP chick. Shit man, she was writing me a ticket, right, but I told myself 'fuck it man.' That's when I got the cajones to tell her, 'Ma'am, I'm sorry I was speeding, but I have to tell you, you have the nicest black hair I've ever seen.' And it was true, man. Anyway Frenchy, lemme cut to the chase—I got a date with that MP chick that same night. I took her out to a club, man. Yep, sure did. Hell, that ticket she wrote me was just a written warning anyway. When she gave it to me, I asked for her phone number—that was after I told her about her gorgeous black hair. Anyway, she gave me her phone number, and I called her that night. Took her out too. Had me a great time. Yep, sure did."

All Boudreau could think of saying was, "That's interesting."

* * *

Fifteen minutes later, the taxi cab reached the front gate of Fort Benjamin Harrison.

"Don't worry, stud," the cab driver reassured Boudreau, "I know exactly where the DINFOS Student Company barracks is."

"What's DINFOS?" Boudreau immediately asked. He had never heard the term.

"Shit, stud—you college boys. I don't know about you college types sometimes," said the driver. "Frenchy, DINFOS is your AIT, man. Stands for Defense Information School."

Boudreau nodded in approval and said, "Oh, I see. Thanks."

The cab driver was now driving slowly and carefully observing the surroundings. He took a quick left then the second right.

"Uh—yep—yep, it's down this road here," he said. "I remember this part of the base. Heh, who knows Frenchy? Maybe I'll see that MP chick again. I promise not to speed though."

Boudreau, remaining quiet, kept looking at the buildings.

"Uh, yeah, there it is," said the cab driver, pointing. "DINFOS Student Company." He pulled the cab into the front driveway.

"Need any help with your bags, Frenchy?"

"Nah, Mike, I'm good to go, but thanks." Boudreau removed a five dollar bill from his wallet and gave it to the cab driver.

"Hey thanks, Frenchy. Fort Ben pays us for these trips, but I always appreciate a tip."

"Sure, no problem," replied Boudreau as he got out of the cab and proceeded to remove his two duffle bags.

"Hey by the way, Frenchy, here's that paper I've got to have you sign. And here's my card too, man."

Boudreau, fumbling with the duffle bags on the back seat, reached with his right hand, and took the paper from the driver. The driver handed him a pen.

"Just sign at the bottom, Frenchy."

Boudreau signed the paper and gave him back the paper and the pen.

"And again, stud, here's my card."

Boudreau took the business card and gave it a cursory look.

The Gents Club. Two Drink Minimum.

The business card was light pink in color with black lettering.

"Come check out the action sometime, Frenchy."

Chapter Forty-Four

Boudreau walked through two metal doors and entered the student barracks building.

Nice, he thought, as he peered down the hallway. *Much nicer than our barracks back in Basic.* He looked at his watch. It was minutes shy of seven thirty PM. He then looked to his right and noticed a soldier manning a work desk. He walked to the desk and placed his duffle bags on the beige tile floor, a tile floor that had a recently-buffed look to it.

"I'm Private Reynolds," said the soldier manning the desk. He was wearing his BDUs and sitting on a gray metal chair. "You must be a new student. Can I help you?"

"Yes," said Boudreau. "I'm Specialist Boudreau. I'm here for the journalism AIT."

"Print or broadcasting?" asked Reynolds.

"Print," responded Boudreau as he sized up Reynolds. He guessed the young private couldn't be older than twenty.

"Print—that's cool," Reynolds said. "I'll need a copy of your orders, specialist."

Boudreau unsnapped the top portion of the duffle bag nearest him. He removed a pair of running shoes and a copy of Capote's *In Cold Blood.*

There, he thought, as he fumbled with some clothing items. *My orders—in that manila folder.* He opened the folder and handed a copy of his orders to Reynolds.

"You'll like it here, specialist," Reynolds said as he placed Boudreau's orders in a metal tray occupying the desk. "It's a joint school—all branches are here: Army, Navy, Air Force, Marines. We even have Coast Guard students and civilian government employees here."

"Great," said Boudreau in an upbeat way. "I'm looking forward to it."

"We Army students here do PT five days a week. Nobody else does that," said Reynolds. He started filling out a log form. "But academics are stressed here. It's a tough MOS. About a third of the students get recycled. Some, if they keep failing, get to pick another MOS."

Hmmn, thought Boudreau, concerned. *Just what I need. A tough academic program. Academics' never been my strong point.*

Reynolds kept filling out the paperwork. "Specialist Boudreau, I'm gonna inprocess you now. Won't take more than five minutes. I'll sign you out linen and assign you a room. I'd love to give you a single room, but I can't—everybody gets paired up."

"No problem," replied Boudreau. "I understand." He started closing and locking up his open duffle bag.

"Next available room is Room 128," continued Reynolds. "You're with Parker. He's so-so. Parties a lot like some other students here. He's been recycled once, which means academic probation, which means no privileges. He's a cool dude, though. He sure likes his David Bowie music too."

Reynolds stapled some papers together and then he removed another form from a different metal tray.

"All right, specialist, just sign here," he said. He handed Boudreau a pen. "I'll give you the keys to your room, too."

Boudreau took the pen and signed the form.

"Room 128 is on the right, down the hallway. I think it's the fifth room on the right," Reynolds said. He handed Boudreau a set of keys, a pillow, and some linen.

"Thanks," said Boudreau. He grabbed his duffle bags and started walking down the hallway.

* * *

Room 128 was indeed the fifth room on the right. Boudreau turned the doorknob and discovered the room was locked. He unlocked it, flipped on the lights, and stepped inside. He immediately noticed a David Bowie poster next to a mirror on the right side of the room.

Guess I'll set up on the left side. He placed his two duffle bags, pillow, and linen on the bottom left bunk and quickly started unpacking. Some five minutes later he heard a fumbling sound—someone fumbling with the doorknob. He walked up to the door and opened it.

"Oh, hmmn? What up, dude?" said a tall lanky guy wearing faded blue jeans and a white T-shirt. The T-shirt had a picture of David Bowie's face on the front side.

"Guess I can't have this room all to myself. You must be my new roommate. Name's Tom Parker."

"Specialist Boudreau. Nice meeting you." They shook hands. Parker entered the room.

"So, are you print or broadcasting?" Parker asked as he sat on his bunk.

"Print," said Boudreau as he walked back to his duffle bags and resumed unpacking them.

"Thirsty any, Jack? I am," said Parker. He started walking toward a brown mini refrigerator that occupied the back center portion of the room.

"Nah, I'm good, Tom. Thanks."

Parker reached down, opened the refrigerator door, and grabbed a can of Dr. Pepper. He shut the refrigerator door and sat back down on his bunk.

"I think your class starts Thursday, Jack. First thing right off the bat is this fucking grammar test. It ain't a cake walk, bro, just to give you a heads up."

Sweet thought Boudreau. *Just what I need. I suck at tests.* He kept placing clothing items in drawers.

Parker took a sip of Dr. Pepper.

"The print journalism program lasts ten weeks," he said. "It's divided into three programs—journalism, public affairs, and photojournalism—otherwise known as PJ. You'll have a few tests in public affairs, and you have to give a coupla of speeches too. PJ is basically taking photos and developing film. Everybody passes PJ. It starts in week five of DINFOS. Public affairs ain't too bad. I find it boring, and you have to study for those tests, but you'll be okay."

He took another sip from his Dr. Pepper can.

"Dude, let me tell you: the real kicker is journalism," Parker said.

He spoke fast and with a sense of purpose.

"Journalism and public affairs both last the entire ten weeks. The tough part about journalism is the attention to detail. Misspellings and grammar mistakes—that shit can kill you, Jack. Some students also struggle with sports writing, but not too many. The real tough assignments are the feature assignments."

"I see," said Boudreau, absorbing it all while still filling up drawers.

Parker suddenly stood up.

"You hungry, Jack? I've got Doritos next to my work desk here."

"Nah, I'm fine, Tom. Thanks anyway."

Parker walked to his desk that was situated next to his bunk. He opened a drawer and pulled out a bag of Doritos.

"Dude, if your average falls below a seventy, then you get placed on academic probation. Don't mean to scare you any, Jack. I'm just giving you the run-down." He sat back down on the bunk.

Boudreau, still unpacking, said, "I see," but his thoughts quickly shifted to that upcoming grammar test. *I suck at grammar. Editors at the* Bangor Daily News *never told me I was awful, but I know grammar doesn't come easy to me.*

"Most students will do okay up until features. That's the real ass-kicker, Jack," Parker said. He was munching on a Dorito. "That's when the grades and the GPAs start tanking. What else, man? What else can I tell you, Jack? Oh, well, see DINFOS is a joint service school. Ain't no way this place is a level-playing field, buddy, I can tell you that."

"How so?" inquired Boudreau. He stopped unpacking and took a break by sitting on his bunk.

"Dude, we do PT five days a week. Marine Jarheads do it three times a week. Air Force and Navy—beats me. I don't think they do PT."

He took a quick sip of Dr. Pepper.

"Bottom line, Jack, we Army grunts do PT, and we also have room inspections and clean-up details. All of that shit takes time, and time is precious when you have journalism assignments. That's the thing—we Army soldiers have less time to spend on our academics."

"I see," said Boudreau, listening attentively.

"Shit bro, would you believe the Air Force has maid service in their student building?"

"No way," said Boudreau.

"I shit you not, Jack. We have clean-up details, and they have maid service. Fuck man, the Air Force barracks here is the equivalent of a Holiday Inn with maid service."

He paused for a second or two, then he said, "Well, Jack, the best part about this place is the social scene, man. After two weeks, as long as your average is above seventy, then you get privileges—like you're able to go out on weekends and shit."

"I see," said Boudreau, his thoughts again shifting to the grammar test.

"Tons of hot chicks here, Jack. Right now, yours truly is working on this little hot Navy chick. Gorgeous face. Nice rack too."

Boudreau thoughts suddenly shifted to Cindy.

"Yep, she's real fine, Jack, trust me. Anyway, the social scene is real good. Just keep that GPA above seventy, my friend. Sure there's rules here against drinking and sex, but you know the Eleventh Commandment, right?" He turned and looked at Boudreau who was silent.

"Eleventh Commandment, Jack. 'Thou shall not get caught.' That's the key. Hell the drill sergeants and instructors here know we students party. Key is just don't get caught."

"I see," said Boudreau. He quickly thought things over.

"See, Tom, I'm not really a partier. To tell you the truth, I'm not one to break the rules or anything. Plus my fiancé and I broke up about a month ago—actually she broke it off. I'm not sure if I'm ready to check the marketplace right now. Know what I mean?"

"Ah, Jack. You're a Boy Scout, man. Take the plunge," Parker said, smiling. "Sorry to hear about your breakup, but there's plenty of chicks out here."

He took another quick sip of Dr. Pepper. "Shit Jack, there's this one chick here, right. This skinny blond girl. She's in the Navy. Word is she was a stripper before joining the Navy. Anyway, she went hard for our Army First Sergeant here, a black, muscular dude by the name of Jones. He looks like Marvelous Marvin Hagler—you know, the boxer."

"Yeah," said Boudreau. "I follow boxing some. Hagler was one of the best."

"Right. Well, Navy blond chick and Jones hit it off, right, and have this fling, and now Jones's in deep shit 'cause he's married. Rumor has it the Army's chaptering his ass out. And his wife is filing for divorce, too. Anyway, Jack, Jones got his ass replaced by First Sergeant Rose just a couple of days ago. Rose's a real soldier, man. He's the real deal. All tabbed out: airborne, air assault, former drill sergeant, Ranger. Tall, muscular dude."

"Oh," said Boudreau, nodding his head, showing he was following the conversation.

"So, we got First Sergeant Rose," Parker said.

He was back to chewing on a Dorito chip.

"Then we have two drill sergeants, both of whom made it through DINFOS as students some years back. One dude's last name is Benoit. Drill Sergeant Benoit. He was a broadcasting instructor here. Real nice guy. The other drill sergeant is a nice looking Army chick. Drill Sergeant Harper. Looks like a shorter version of Jamie Lee Curtis. She's currently dating some Marine recruiter stationed in downtown Indy. Harper's hot, bro. I'd do her. Anyway, the point is there's plenty of pussy here at DINFOS."

CHAPTER FORTY-FIVE

While Boudreau was getting ready to start his academic training at DINFOS, Boros and his Boys got word from L.D. about an upcoming drug shipment.

"This would be a huge one," L.D. had told Boros and his crew on a weekday night. L.D. had suggested they all meet at Leavenworth's 2010 Club because L.D. never spoke about such business matters over the phone.

"Not weed but coke this time, fellas. Sizeable load, dudes. Destination's Denver. I'm finalizing the details."

"How much?" inquired Boros. "What's our cut? Our slice?" He was sitting in a puffy lounge chair, nursing a Corona. Jackson, Carlos, and Jose sat behind him.

"Twenty-five big ones," said L.D.

Boros quickly did the math. *That's ten grand to me, five grand for each of my Boys.*

"And I got what you requested too," said L.D. matter-of-factly. He took a quick sip from his rum and Coke. "Remember what we talked about, B? About the stuff you need for protection?"

"Yeah," said Boros, shifting in his chair. "When are we getting those?"

"Tonight. Right here in the parking lot. How about it, B? If I close the Denver deal, are you and your boys gonna move it?"

"Sure L.D. You can count on us," Boros said, smiling. "Plus it's Lots Dough, right?"

CHAPTER FORTY-SIX

"**W**hat the fuck, man," Parker said. He was lying on his bunk, munching on a Dorito chip. He was reacting to someone fumbling with the door. Boudreau remained silent. What came next was the sound of someone inserting a key in the doorknob.

"What the?"

The door opened, and a young soldier dressed in his Class A uniform and carrying two Army duffle bags was standing in the entrance.

"Hi. I'm Private Brian Keller. I just got assigned to this room."

"You're shitting me, right?" said Parker, propping himself off the bunk.

"Nope. Guy at the front desk assigned me to this room and gave me a room key. He also told me Private Parker was moving out soon to another room."

"That would be me," said Parker. "I guess that's what happens to a lot of us recycles—we get reassigned to another room. Who knows, maybe I'll get relocated on the second floor where that Navy chick hangs out."

Boudreau stood up. "Hi, I'm Specialist Jack Boudreau. Unfortunately, there's only two desks and two mirrors here, but we can share my side of the room till Parker moves out."

"That'll work," said Keller. He stepped inside the room and placed his duffle bags next to Boudreau's bunk.

"So Keller, where you coming from?" asked Parker. He sat back down on his bunk. "Where'd you do Basic?"

"Fort Jackson, South Carolina."

"Fort Fucking Jackson," said Parker.

He sat down on his bunk again, interlaced his hands behind his head, and stared at the ceiling.

"That place sucks, man. It's where I did Basic too."

Keller started unpacking while Boudreau took a seat behind the small work desk on his side of the room.

A few quiet seconds passed, so to break the silence Boudreau said, "Parker, why don't you give Keller the run-down about this place; tell him what you told me about DINFOS," and that's when Parker began mentioning the things he had previous told Boudreau—the upcoming grammar test, the unlevel playing field, the importance of a GPA of at least a seventy, the DINFOS social scene. Keller, busy unpacking, listened attentively and chimed in with occasional questions.

* * *

Twenty minutes later, there was a knock at the door. Keller was just wrapping up his unpacking. Boudreau stood up and opened the door.

"Late-night formation for the newbies."

It was Private Reynolds.

"I just got word that there'll be a formation for the new arrivals right next to the CQ desk in fifteen mikes. Uniform is whatever—Class As are okay, but you can wear civvies, too."

"Thanks Reynolds," said Boudreau, still holding the doorknob. "Roger that. Keller and I will be there."

Boudreau and Keller changed into civilian attire. Both put on jeans and short-sleeved shirts. Parker, still lying on his bunk and staring at the ceiling, was now listening to his Walkman.

"You dudes have fun," he said loudly to compensate for the music emanating from his earphones. "And give me a good scouting report, fellas. I wanna know if there's any hotties in your class."

* * *

"Platoon—attention!" said the middle-aged man at the head of the formation.

Boudreau and Keller were in the third squad of the four-squad platoon. The platoon, consisting of no more than thirty members, had formed up near Reynold's work desk in four even lines. The middle-aged man, sporting a military-cropped moustache, addressed them.

"At—ease. I'm Sergeant Foster, your DINFOS platoon leader. I'm a broadcasting student here, and I've been here for about four weeks now. And though I'm a colleague of yours, you will address me as sergeant."

Boudreau sized up Foster and guessed he was in his mid-forties. He noticed Foster's face was weathered and wrinkled some, and that his hairline was receding.

Foster's got an intense look to him, he thought.

"As your platoon sergeant, I'm one of your bosses," said Foster, authoritatively. "The chain of command here is simple: if you have a problem, see your squad leader; if that doesn't work out, then see me. I'm in Room 135. If I can't help you out, then see one of the drill sergeants."

Foster quickly scanned the formation.

"Two other students here at DINFOS are sergeants. Sergeant Miller, please raise your hand to be recognized."

A blond, heavyset man in the first squad raised his hand.

"Another sergeant here is Sergeant Caulkins," Foster said. "Sergeant Caulkins, please raise your hand to be recognized."

A middle-aged man with dark-brown hair raised his hand. He too was standing in the first squad.

"DINFOS Student Company," said Foster, "how about a round of applause for Sergeant Caulkins, who recently returned here after a combat tour in the Persian Gulf."

Polite applause ensued, and Caulkins again raised his hand as an acknowledgement.

"So you have three sergeants as fellow students here," continued Foster. "You will give us our proper respect and courtesies as NCOs. Now, a couple of minor things to cover before I turn it over to First Sergeant Rose.

Boudreau thought: *Rose must be that big guy standing behind Foster.*

"Our company commander is Captain Pierce. You won't see her here too often, but if you should see her—or any other officer—then don't forget to render a proper salute. DINFOS might be an academic environment, but we can't forget about our soldier training, about drill and ceremony stuff. Salute officers when you see them," Foster said. "And one last thing before I turn it over to our first sergeant. I'm a fair guy, gang, and if I can help you, I will. But don't play games with me. I'm forty-six years old, I've been there and done that—Vietnam vet, married, then divorced, coupla kids, went bankrupt, then I straightened out my finances, was active-duty, then National Guard, now I'm in the Army Reserves. You name it; I've done it or seen it. I'm an actor by training—I've done some B-movies and the like—and I can read people very well, so don't play games with me. I do broadcasting as my civilian job, and now I'm getting broadcasting training for my slot in a Reserve unit. Got a problem—come see me."

Foster again scanned the formation.

"Okay, DINFOS Student Company. Let me turn it over to our First Sergeant. Top?"

The tall, muscular man standing behind Foster took three steps forward. He was wearing a tight-fitting T-shirt, faded jeans that were also worn tightly, and cowboy boots that were light brown in color. Boudreau noticed Rose had a can of snuff in one of his front pockets.

"I'm First Sergeant Rose. I want to welcome you all to DINFOS," said the big man in a confident voice. He cleared his throat.

"There's no secret about it folks, this is a tough school, and not every student makes the cut. That's life. Failure is part of life sometimes, so get used to it. Yes, we'll do PT during the work week, and yes, we'll do some CTT training, and then an FTX towards the end of this ten-week course, but the bottom line gang is this: this is an academic school to train you to be a print journalist or a broadcast journalist. That means your main job here is to study, work hard, and pass this school. You're here to hit the books, gang, so good luck with that."

Rose crossed his muscular arms and assessed the formation before him.

"As for myself, my background's infantry. I'm a grunt. Airborne, air assault, Ranger, Drill Sergeant School—I did all that high-speed grunt stuff. But four years ago, I decided to change my MOS. Frankly, I got tired of the field stuff with bugs crawling up my ass. I knew I liked to read, and yeah, I'm sorta bookish, so I decided to try my hand at journalism. Why am I telling you all this story? The reason is simple—I made it through here. I passed this school, and if I can do it, then I'm confident you guys can make it. Do what it takes folks—that's a tip from me to you. If you need to pull an all-nighter, then pull a fucking all-nighter. Do your best, gang— that's all you can do. Drill Sergeants Harper and Benoit, they too made it through this course, so we're here to help you. So do your best, and don't break down. A couple of years back, we had a broadcasting student here who was failing the course and committed suicide in part because he was failing. We don't need that shit here. A course like this ain't worth doing something like that. You fail, you'll get recycled. You fail again, then you get to pick another MOS and try something else. So don't break down, okay? Can I get a hooah on that?"

"Hooah" replied the students in formation, and just then, just as he finished saying his "hooah," Boudreau realized roughly half of the students in formation were girls. *Parker will like this.*

Rose continued. "Folks, I'm not here to scare anyone of you. I'm just putting all the cards out on the table. This is actually a fun place. You'll learn a lot, and you'll make friends."

He paused momentarily. It seemed like he was gathering his thoughts. He looked up at the ceiling, then down at the floor before him.

"Now another thing to discuss is the fact that DINFOS is a joint-service school. Yes, we have Marines, and sailors, and airmen here. We do have Coast Guard members and Department of Defense civilians too. Now, am I going to tell you that it's a level-playing field? Hell no, because it ain't. No question about it, gang, we Army grunts have it hardest. You'll have more to do than your counterparts and less time to do it in. Yes we'll have some inspections; yes we'll PT; yes we'll do a bit of CTT training. None of the other services will do those things save the few and the proud Marines. And as an Army First Sergeant you know what I'm gonna tell you— suck it up and drive on. An unlevel playing field is sometimes part of life too. Everyone of you could have gone to the Air Force recruiter or the Navy recruiter or whatever. But you didn't. You went to the Army recruiter, and your ass signed up with the Army. Live with it, gang."

He paused again. Boudreau, careful not to lock his knees, moved his feet and legs slightly to loosen them up.

"After two weeks here, we high-speed cadre will give you guys privileges so long as your academic average is at least a seventy. This means you'll be able to go out on weekends so long as your ass is back here in these barracks by 1800 hours on Sundays. Now some more rules. The use of tobacco and of alcohol is prohibited at DINFOS. If you're a smoker, too bad. Even if you're of legal age, you can't drink alcohol here. No tobacco, no alcohol. Also, no pornography, and no sex either. The only exception to the no-sex rule is if you're married, then you can have sex with your spouse if your spouse is visiting you. Those are the rules."

Rose coughed to clear his throat. "Now just because I make the coffee doesn't mean I drink it, gang. I don't make these rules, but I do enforce them. When the cadre and I do our inspections, we better not find any porno magazines. We also better not find any smokes or booze. Now, like Sergeant Foster said about himself, I, too, have been around; I, too, have been there and done that. I'm a straight shooter, gang, and I ain't no hypocrite. Yes, I use tobacco—I like to chew it. Yes, I consume alcohol, and yes, as a divorced bachelor, I chase pussy. I have two favorite types of music – country and western. That's me, folks. Here's the thing—I can do all that stuff, but you guys can't. Rules apply for students, not the cadre. That's just the way it is. Just be good little boys and girls for ten weeks, then these rules won't apply anymore."

Rose again cleared his throat.

"Now, am I stupid enough to believe that on weekends you guys won't smoke, drink, or do the wild thing? Hell no, but that still doesn't give you license to do that stuff. All I can tell you guys is if you decide to push the envelope, then just make sure you don't break the seal. Don't break the rules, gang. If so, I promise you, there will be consequences. Break one of these rules and you're looking at an Article 15. That shit don't look good on your military record, particularly since you're still in AIT. Break the rules, gang, then live with the consequences. And yes, don't be surprised if you discover that I and the cadre here check out bars and hotels where some of your past counterparts decided to get creative. We'll do our rounds—don't let us catch you at bars. Now, one last thing before I dismiss you all for the evening. If your creative ass decides to break these rules, then by all means don't drink and drive. Drinking alcohol in and of itself is a rule violation, but don't make it fucking worse by driving on top of that. Also, if you decide to get your cock or pussy wet, then make sure you've got protection. Sex is a DINFOS rule violation, but getting someone pregnant muddies the water even further. 'Course my idea of safe sex is having both feet on the ground, that way I have better traction to do what I'm doing, but you know what I mean by safe sex. Make sure the cock has that rubber protective coat on it. Are we tracking DINFOS Student Company?"

"Hooah," replied the students.

"Good," said Rose. He then ordered, "Platoon – attention!" and all the students snapped to the position of attention.

"Good luck to you all," said Rose. "You all have a grammar test in less than forty-eight hours, so good luck on that too. Dismissed!"

CHAPTER FORTY-SEVEN

*C*rap, thought Boudreau. *Hmm? Jeez. I think... I think C looks like the best answer. Yeah, it's C.*

He circled the letter C option of his grammar test.

Proper use of commas; what's wrong with this sentence? Proper us of colons and semicolons; capitalization; differences between to, too, and two; their versus there versus they're; who versus whom versus who's; that versus which; hear versus here; where versus wear; effect versus affect; lite versus light; different verb tenses—

Damn I hate exams. He was forty minutes into the grammar test. *One hundred questions, and I can only miss thirty. When I wrote articles at the* Bangor Daily News, *I always had my AP Stylebook with me, but now the test rules don't allow me to use references. Crap.*

* * *

Boudreau stood up. He picked up his exam answer sheet and booklet and his number two pencil, and then he started walking to the front of the classroom to turn in his grammar exam.

Well, I've done the best I could, he thought as he walked quietly. He glanced at his watch. It was minutes shy of ten AM.

"How'd you do, Jack?" asked Keller as soon as Boudreau exited the classroom. Keller, who had finished the same test ten minutes prior, was waiting for his roommate in the hallway.

"Oh, I never know with these things," said Boudreau, concern written all over his face. "You know, Brian, you would think this shit would be easy for a former civilian reporter such as yours truly, but grammar never came easy to me. I don't have a clue, Brian. What did you think of the exam?"

"Not a cake walk, that's for sure, but I think I came out on top. Rumor has it the test results will be posted around noon."

"Well, I guess that's a good thing," said Boudreau as the two started walking down the wide hallway. "We'll know soon enough then."

To kill time, Boudreau and Keller, like most of the new DINFOS students, decided to grab a bite to eat at the nearby mess hall, located just two buildings away from the DINFOS classroom building.

* * *

"What did you guys think of that fucker, huh?" said an Army soldier standing in front of Keller. He had turned around to ask the question. The lunch line was maybe thirty students deep. Keller and Boudreau, who had just arrived at the mess hall, were the last two in the queue.

"Name's Dan Smith. Standing next to me is Paula Morris. I saw you guys in that grammar test classroom. Hell of an exam, huh?"

"Challenging," said Keller. Boudreau nodded in agreement. The four Army soldiers shook hands as the line slowly moved forward.

"Got that right, buddy," said Smith, still referring to the exam. He had the same height and build as Boudreau (5'7", 165 pounds), but he had the start of a receding hairline, and his mouth seemed to always sport a smile.

"Challenging to say the least. That exam kicked my butt. I'll definitely take a seventy and be happy," he said, speaking in a quick, excited voice. "See boys—and by the way, I consider you one of the boys, Paula—see, I don't want to get fucking recycled."

"Oh, Dan," Morris said, smiling at him. Her hand touched his thigh. "None of us want to get recycled."

"Yeah, but especially me," Smith said, smiling back at her. He turned to look at Keller and Boudreau.

"See, me and my fiancé—her name's Tina—planned our wedding for early September, right after this course ends. If I get recycled, that's really screwing the pooch. I'll be lost in the sauce. I'll be fucked, man."

No one said anything. Boudreau thought of Cindy momentarily; Morris, no longer smiling, looked down at the floor.

The food line kept moving slowly. Boudreau, uncomfortable that no one had said a thing for some ten seconds, decided to break the ice.

"I hope this place is still serving breakfast," he said, to which Morris replied:

"I think they are. I see some trays with breakfast items."

Smith chimed in with, "Breakfast, that sounds great."

He winked at Morris. She smiled back at him.

In ten minutes the foursome had their food items on their large trays. They each filled their glasses with drinks, and then they sat at a small table near the large salad bar occupying the center of the mess hall.

"This mess hall's pretty squared away," Smith said shortly after he sat down next to Morris. He had ordered scrambled eggs, bacon, and biscuits and gravy. "Better than Basic at Fort Jackson, that's for sure."

"Roger that," Keller said. "Jackson wasn't bad mess hall-wise, but this place rocks in comparison."

More chit chat by the foursome that lasted for some ten minutes, then at one point Morris got up and said, "I'm getting a refill on my Coke. Anyone need anything?"

"Nah, baby doll," Smith said, winking at her.

Keller and Boudreau said they were okay. Morris headed for the soda machines.

"Check her out, dudes—she's fine isn't she?" said Smith as Morris walked away. He sipped from his glass of orange juice. He was smiling too.

"Yes, she is," said Keller. "Morris's a cute blond." Boudreau just nodded in approval.

"A little heavy in the butt region, but I like a little junk in the trunk—know what I mean. A little cushion for the pushing always helps."

Keller laughed. Boudreau smiled. Keller then cleared his throat.

"But Smith, man, you're engaged right? You ain't thinking of hooking up with Morris, are you?"

"Don't be such a Boy Scout, Keller," said Smith, smiling. "What happens at DINFOS stays at DINFOS. If opportunity knocks, I'll open the door."

* * *

The results of the grammar exam were posted just before noon on the second floor of the DINFOS classroom building. Smith, Morris, Keller, and Boudreau had all passed with the respective grades of 72, 94, 81 and 82. All new DINFOS students spent the remainder of the afternoon filling out administrative paperwork and receiving a tour of the school library that occupied the bottom floor of the student building. For those students who had passed the exam (80 percent had), the journalism classes would start the next day; for the one-fifth of students who had failed, the start of JPREP (an acronym standing for journalism preparation) would await them the next day.

* * *

When Boudreau and Keller entered their barracks room after dinner that night, they immediately realized Parker had packed his belongings and moved to another room. Gone were Parker's belongings, including his sizeable David Bowie poster that used to hang next to his bunk. Another sign of Parker's departure was

a note, handwritten and scotched-taped to a mirror. Boudreau read the note shortly after entering the room.

Dudes. My new room is upstairs, Room 204. My roommate is PFC Mullins, a cool chap. Good luck with the program. Hope you both passed the grammar test.

Later,
Parker

P.S. I'm now four rooms away from that hot Navy chick. Ca-chung, ca-chung.

P.S.S. Heard your class has some hotties too. I'll be on the lookout.

"Well Jack, do you want Parker's bunk and side of the room, or do you want me to take it?" asked Keller as he too finished reading Parker's note.

"How about we flip for it?" said Boudreau. He removed Parker's note from the mirror.

"Okay," said Keller, then he removed a quarter from his front pocket. "Got a quarter right here. What will it be?"

Without hesitating Boudreau said, "I'll take tails."

Keller flipped the coin and made sure it landed on Parker's bunk.

"Heads, Jack. I win." Boudreau rolled his eyes.

"I'll stay put," said Keller, smiling. "You take Parker's bunk."

"Deal's a deal," said Boudreau. He scrunched Parker's letter and threw it in a nearby metal wastebasket.

"And I've got another deal for you, Jack."

"I'm all ears," said Boudreau.

"Bet you ten bucks Smith and Morris will 'do it' before this course ends. They'll knock boots, man. I'm sure of it."

"You're on," said Boudreau.

The two shook hands to seal the deal. Boudreau thought *I think Smith's more steam than fire; more talk than action.*

173

CHAPTER FORTY-EIGHT

B oudreau took one last bite to finish off his oatmeal raisin cookie. He took a sip of water to wash it down; then, he browsed through parts of his outline for his planned novel.

Barracks inspection— funny. Murdock's inspection unpassable

Greyhound Bus to Indy

Cab to DINFOS. Cabby's a Pacer's fan. Big dude. Bouncer at titty bar

Roommates—Parker and Keller

Clique is me, Keller, Smith, and Morris

He penciled in, *Write about Platoon Sergeant Foster and Top. Rose. Rules of Engagement include no booze, no tobacco, and no sex*

He went back to reading some entries:

Grammar Test— passed

Keller's bet that Smith and Morris do the wild thing. I didn't buy it.

He closed his notebook.

I've got plenty to write, he thought. *Outline is getting more and more thorough. I think I once read that John Irving writes extremely detailed outlines so that once he starts writing, the novel essentially writes itself.*

He looked at his watch.

Carlos should be here in eighty mikes or so. I hope he answers my questions.

He took another sip of water.

Okay, time for some more inspiration. Just flip to any passage of Capote's In Cold Blood.

He opened *In Cold Blood* to page 154. Midway on the page was the start of another chapter. He started reading the first paragraph of that chapter:

It was midday deep in the Mojave Desert. Perry, sitting on a straw suitcase, was playing a harmonica. Dick was standing at the side of a black-surfaced highway, Route 66, his eyes fixed upon the immaculate emptiness as though the fervor of his gaze could force motorists to materialize. Few did, and none of those stopped for the hitchhikers. One truck driver, bound for Needles, California, had offered a lift, but ...

CHAPTER FORTY-NINE

"**W**ell we might as well get started."
Tech Sergeant Mike McNeil, an eighteen-year Air Force veteran and one of four journalism instructors at DINFOS, was sitting on one of the corners of his massive wooden desk that occupied the front portion of the classroom. Behind him was a large black chalkboard, and slightly to his left was a small-screen television set situated atop a metal transport cart that could be wheeled away. Sixteen students, representing the four military branches and the Coast Guard, were in the classroom. Each student sat behind a cream-colored desk that in part served as a support platform for a Brother computer. Morris, Keller, and Boudreau sat next to each other (Keller behind Boudreau, Morris to Boudreau's right). Smith, to his dismay, had been assigned to another journalism classroom under a different instructor.

"Good morning. I'm Tech Sergeant McNeil, your journalism instructor." McNeil, a short forty-year old with dirty blond hair and an expressive face, was an enthused, passionate sort who spoke rapidly.

"Congrats on passing the grammar test. You guys can relax for today—I won't assign homework this morning, and no one needs to take notes as well. Just everybody relax and listen to my introductory talk."

Boudreau, relieved there wouldn't be an upcoming assignment, turned to Morris and gave her a thumbs up. She smiled and gave a thumbs up of her own.

"I'll be talking about the course, my expectations, and my grading policy. In case you haven't noticed, I'm a laid-back kind of guy, but having said that, when it's time to work, we work, okay? I'm very serious about deadlines, gang. A deadline is a deadline is a deadline. I've got a stopwatch, and my deadlines are down to the second. I'll give you all a five-minute warning before an assignment is due, but never turn in a late assignment."

McNeil proceeded to guide his feet to the floor. He stood up and walked to his black leather swivel chair that was behind his massive desk. He took a seat in the chair.

"Now I won't lie to you guys—this course is challenging, but don't freak out on me, okay? There's no need to hit the panic button here," he said in a reassuring tone. "Just do as I say. Do your best, work hard, and follow my instructions. If you do that, I'm confident all of you will do okay in this course."

He drummed his left fingers on the desk for a few seconds as he scanned the classroom of new students.

"Some good news," McNeil said. "The last class I taught, not one student failed. I'm hoping the same will happen with this class."

He drummed his fingers again on the big desk.

"There are three subjects in this DINFOS course: journalism, public affairs, and photo journalism. Simply put, gang, this specific course—the journalism course—is the ass kicker. Don't slack off on public affairs and PJ, but none of you will have difficulty with those courses. The tough one is this one, and that's where I come in. Just follow my instructions, okay?"

Every student was listening attentively to McNeil. Some nodded their heads, agreeing with what he was saying.

"The key to this class is to copyedit your work. Copyedit, copyedit, copyedit," he said. "I can't say copyediting enough. No one gets it right the first time, gang. Even Hemingway went through many drafts before he submitted his manuscripts for publication. By the way, Hemingway got his start as a reporter. Did any of you know that?"

None of the students spoke. Boudreau knew Hemingway started out as a journalist, but he chose not to speak up.

McNeil continued. "So copyediting's the key. Misspellings, grammar mistakes, poor paragraph transitions—I gotta take points off for those, especially misspellings. Misspell a name and it's minus fifty points right off the bat. That means the highest grade you can get is a fifty. Don't misspell a name, okay?"

Again no student spoke.

McNeil leaned back in his chair.

"A few additional things. You can bring small food items in this classroom, but not meals. No burgers, fries—food items like that. You can eat a chocolate bar in here and that's okay, but just make sure you all police after yourselves. Don't leave trash around; use the wastebasket. You can always bring your drinks in here too. Preferably you'll have a lid on your drink, otherwise, your drink rests on the floor so it won't spill on your computer keyboard. We can't afford to have any of you spill a drink on one of the computers. Those are the rules, gang. No drinks on your desk unless your drink is capped or has a lid. What else? Oh, as you can see, we have a television set in this classroom."

He pointed to his left.

"There will be some study time in here, and some break time too, and when we have those then we can watch TV, but here's the catch: the only authorized channel is CNN News. You're all aspiring to become military journalists, so we have to follow the news. News is our business, gang. That's what we can watch on television."

He paused and asked if there were any questions. There were none.

"You guys are too quiet. No questions? Okay. Well, each and every one of you here will learn how to write headlines, leads, bridges, news stories, sport stories, and feature stories. That's what this course is about. No doubt about it gang, features is what separates the men from the boys. Inevitably, that's where your GPA will head south, but again, just do as I say and you should be okay. What else?"

He looked up at the ceiling for a few seconds, gathering his thoughts.

"Oh yeah, grades. Minus fifty for a misspelled name. The other errors vary from minus one to minus ten points. What I call a minor error in fact is minus five points. A major error in fact brings you down ten points. Grammar mistakes and transition problems are usually minus three to minus five points. Remember to save all your work on your computer, and to spell-check everything. Attention to detail is key in this business.

"What else? What else?" said McNeil. He rubbed his chin with his right hand.

"Oh yeah, uh, the final project here at DINFOS is called *Final Cut*. During *Final Cut* you're part of a team that puts together your very own newspaper. Some of you will be editors, some of you will be reporters and photographers, and some of you will also do the newspaper layout of the articles and photographs. *Final Cut* is fun, a lot of work, and very rewarding. You'll be part of a team and receive a team grade for your efforts."

He paused again.

"And one last thing gang, and this is important. We journalists write at the ninth-grade reading level. Check it out: the *New York Times*, *USA Today*, the *Washington Post*, the *Indianapolis Star*—read their articles; it's all at the ninth-grade reading level. This DINFOS course will train you on how not to write long sentences and on why we don't use big words. Journalism is short sentences, gang, not long sentences. We write to be understood. We write for our general reading public. Again, journalists write at the ninth-grade reading level. A conflagration took place—no, we don't write like that. Write 'a fire broke out'. The driver was operating his motor vehicle—oh no, we don't write that. Write 'the driver drove his car.' She was a concubine. Hell no. Write instead 'She was a mistress.' Nothing fancy with our words, gang, and no long sentences either. Now

Paul Bouchard

I know many of you have college educations or at least some college, but you have to keep in mind that journalists write for the general public. It does you no good to write conflagration when you mean a fire."

CHAPTER FIFTY

Boros and his Boys were in Denver. They had agreed to transport the big shipment for L.D., and now they were looking for the street where the warehouse—the site of the drop off—was supposed to be. Jose and Carlos were in the lead vehicle, the trunk of which had the cocaine; Boros and Jackson were in the recon car, following closely and communicating with Jose and Carlos via cell phones.

"Next right, next right," Boros instructed from the passenger seat of the second car, the car that was driven by Jackson and trailing Jose's lead vehicle by maybe a dozen car lengths. "Carlos—tell Jose to take the next right."

"Roger, boss. 'Hey Jose – boss says it's the next right.'"

Jose flipped on the turn signal and took the next right, and just as Jackson was about to do the same to take the following right he saw flashing blue lights in his rearview mirror.

"We got trouble, boss," he said to Boros. "Pigs right behind us; their lights flashing."

"Stay cool, bro, stay cool," Boros said, calmly.

He reached in and felt around the right pocket of his jacket. He felt his 9mm handgun. It was loaded, but not cocked.

"Just pullover and stay cool, Jackson. You're the driver, so the pig will ask you questions. If you get into a pickle, I'll cough. That's the cue to let me take over and do the talking."

Jackson pulled the car to the curb. Jose's and Carlos's lead vehicle was no longer in sight.

"License and registration please," said the police officer. He was standing on the car's driver side, flashing a flashlight inside the car. Jackson had his window rolled down. The police officer looked to be in his late forties or early fifties. He was tall and overweight, and he had a thick brown mustache that had early signs of graying.

"Yes sir. Yes officer," Jackson said politely. He opened the car's glove compartment, fumbled a bit for the registration paperwork, and handed the papers to the cop. He then reached back for his wallet, opened it up, and pulled out both his Kansas driver's license and also his military i.d.

"Well gentlemen, the reason I stopped you guys is to inform you that your left taillight ain't functional; it's not working."

"Oh," said Jackson, both surprised and relieved. "Sorry about that officer. I didn't know. I'll be sure to get it fixed as soon as possible."

"That's good," said the policeman. "And may I ask what you two boys from Kansas are doing here in Denver?"

Boros immediately coughed and said, "Oh, sir, we're just visiting friends for the weekend."

"I see," said the police officer as he looked at Jackson's license. "Say, I see you're in the Army, Mr. Jackson. And your friend also has a short, military-style haircut. You both military?"

"Yes sir, yes officer," Jackson said, even more relieved. "We're both in the Army."

"Fort Riley, I take it," said the police officer, referring to the large Army installation around Manhattan, Kansas. "You boys part of the Big Red One? I did a tour there myself back in my younger days."

"Oh, no, officer," Jackson said reassuringly. "We're both stationed at Fort Leavenworth."

"Oh, I see," said the officer.

He smiled and handed Jackson his license, military i.d., and car registration.

"Well, you get that taillight fixed now you hear. And I personally thank you both for your military service to our country."

CHAPTER FIFTY-ONE

Boudreau, Keller, Morris, and Smith were eating sandwiches and chips at the DINFOS Snack Bar just down the hallway from McNeil's journalism classroom. It was noon time, and the four were discussing their next speeches—slated for the following week—for their public-affairs DINFOS course. They were seated at a corner table. The Snack Bar, as usual during the lunch hour rush, was packed with DINFOS students.

"What's your next speech gonna be about, Dan?" Morris asked Smith. They were seated next to each other, across the table from Keller and Boudreau.

"Oh I'm thinking about doing something on gays in the military," he said.

Morris looked directly at him. "Are you serious, Dan? That's a sensitive, not to mention controversial, topic."

"Hey, I can handle it, Paula baby. It's good to pick something hot and in the news. President Clinton's Don't Ask Don't Tell policy—What is it? What does it mean? How is it being implemented? I think there's a lot there I can work with."

He started chewing on a potato chip.

"And what about you, honey bun? What's your speech gonna be about?"

"Oh, I don't know, Dan," she said, smiling at him. "I'm thinking of doing something about women in the Army. The whole history of it—World War II, Korea, Vietnam, now the Persian Gulf Conflict."

"And what about you two stud muffins?" Smith asked, referring to Keller and Boudreau. Keller was sipping from his soda while Boudreau, already finished with his lunch, was reading the *Wall Street Journal.*

"Something about the Holocaust," Keller said. "I saw Speilberg's *Schindler's List* not too long ago. Powerful movie. It's giving me some ideas."

"That's cool," Smith said. "Jack—what about you? What's your speech gonna be about?"

"I'm thinking about a topic on NATO. I'm like you," Boudreau told Smith. "I want something that's currently in the news. The whole breakup of the Soviet Union, Europe's perspective on NATO and the U.S.'s perspective. There's a lot I can work with."

"Roger that," Smith said. Morris added, "Yeah, that sounds good, Jack. Good luck."

Boudreau then chimed in with, "I just read a good article on that earthquake in Kobe, Japan. Interesting stuff. I can't help but compare it to when we had an earthquake in San Francisco and riots in L.A."

"How do you mean?" inquired Smith.

"Well," said Boudreau. "The article mentioned that there was absolutely no looting in Kobe after the earthquake even though there was ample opportunity for it. Storefronts were wide open and all, but no one stole anything. Reporters interviewed people there, and the residents of Kobe said the very thought of looting didn't enter their minds."

"And?" asked Smith. "Your point is."

"Dan, the point is the exact opposite happened here in the United States. Earthquake hits California and people are looting left and right."

"Yeah well, I'm not defending that Jack," Smith said. "But just remember this: You can't change the world. People want to steal, they'll steal."

Chapter Fifty-Two

"**M**ission accomplished, my Boys."
Boros and his crew had just returned from their big Denver drop off. It was seven PM on a Sunday night, and the four of them were in Boros's barracks room doing their usual— drinking beer and smoking cigarettes. A small folding table with a bowl of popcorn on it stood erect in the smoke-filled room.

"Well done, my Boys. Good job," said Boros just before he took a drag from his Marlboro Light cigarette. He puffed in, then he exhaled in the direction of the cracked open window next to the folding table. It was a hot and humid night, and the outside thick air didn't seem to be sucking out any of the smoke in the room.

"Big fuckin' shipment—well done," he said, repeating himself. He and the Boys all touched beer bottles as a toast.

"Little hiccup with that pig pulling us over, Jackson. Bro— you gotta keep up with the car maintenance my man. Can't be driving around with busted taillights now, can we?" Then Boros said, "No biggie though. You handled it okay."

He took a sip from his Corona.

"Anyway fellas, for our fine work it's twenty-five big ones from Mr. L.D. Scarface. We'll be in some real money soon, fellas."

Another toast ensued, then Jose and Carlos high-fived each other."

I can always use more dinero, man," Jose said, "especially since some hoochie momma bitch back in San Antone hit me for child support last week. Fucking court order and everything, dudes. I'm gonna fight it, but who knows with this shit. Yeah, I banged the ho some time back during some vacation leave, but who the fuck knows if the kid's mine." He took a big gulp from his beer.

Boros, sitting near the cracked window, said, "And remember fellas—no big purchases and shit. We don't flash the cash around. Car speakers, music, and some clothes—that's okay, but no high-priced jewelry and big fancy wheels and hubcaps and shit. We keep everything on the low-down, fellas. L.D. will pay us soon, and everyone will get their cut."

CHAPTER FIFTY-THREE

Boudreau, like many of his classmates, had settled into a routine by the end of the first week of DINFOS. Up at five AM, personal hygiene; put on BDUs, polish the boots; morning formation outside barracks at 0545; uniform and boot inspections by squad leaders; company march to mess hall; breakfast chow; be at DINFOS building by 0715; journalism classes starting at 0730; lunch break from 1130 to 1300 hours; journalism classes from 1300 to 1400; public affairs class from 1400 to 1500; walk back to barracks; change into Army PT uniform; PT from 1600 to 1700; personal hygiene; change into civvies; dinner chow at mess hall or order out pizza, Chinese food, etc., which Boudreau and Keller never did because their finances were so tight; back to the barracks and hit the student computer room (a large classroom within the barracks) to work on assignments; quiet time kicking off at 2200 hours; lights out whenever he wanted or whenever his assignments were done.

That was Boudreau's weekday routine, a routine common to most Army DINFOS students. On weekends, Boudreau worked on assignments, read the *Wall Street Journal* and *Indianapolis Star* for fun, and took daily five-mile jogs. He also occasionally attended Catholic Mass on Sunday mornings at the base chapel.

Boudreau liked his routine, but there was some stress that came with it. There were pressures at DINFOS: graded assignments almost on a daily basis; giving public affairs speeches in front of classmates; being extra careful not to misspell a word or God-forbid someone's name; working fast to make deadlines; keeping up with the workload—all of these added to his stress level. Still, Jack Boudreau was holding his own. His GPA stood at eighty-seven by the end of two weeks. His roommate Keller came in at eighty-nine, while Morris, a one-time journalism major at the University of Texas at Austin, was one of the top DINFOS students. Her GPA hovered around ninety-six. Smith, whose journalism instructor was a tough and demanding retired naval officer, had a GPA of seventy-seven after two weeks at DINFOS.

* * *

Boudreau worked hard at DINFOS, but he didn't "play hard" as a good number of students did. Once privileges kicked in after two weeks, he wasn't one to crash the ever-popular weekend parties with some of his colleagues. His roommate Keller was the same way, and for that matter Smith and Morris didn't party either.

For Boudreau, his thinking was *Why risk the chance of getting caught?*

For Keller, his thinking was governed by a much more practical concern—at twenty, he wasn't of legal drinking age. As for Morris and Smith, they flirted, but nothing more. Smith's fiancé, a local Indiana girl from Bloomington, actually visited her beau every other weekend.

"Dude, I'm gonna win that ten bucks from you," Boudreau reminded Keller one particular Friday night. The roommates had broken tradition by ordering takeout pizza to reward themselves for decent grades (Boudreau a ninety-one, Keller a ninety-three) on their public affairs speeches earlier that afternoon.

"Morris and Smith flirt a lot and are all lovey-dovey, but they won't do it."

"I still got my money on them," Keller said as he wiped some pizza grease off his mouth with a paper towel. "Plus everybody in class is talking about Morris and Smith as a couple, even though Smith's engaged."

CHAPTER FIFTY-FOUR

"**W**hat? Come again. Repeat that last transmission. Whaddaya mean you can't pay us right now?"

Boros and his Boys were in Boros's barracks room. Boros, on his cell phone, was listening to L.D. on the other end. It was a Wednesday night, and Boros couldn't believe what he was hearing.

"Well, B., it's like this—I'm having cash flow problems right now and—"

"Cash flow problems!" Boros yelled, practically screaming in the phone. "That cash better be flowing in my direction, bro, or you'll definitely be having some problems."

"Look B., I know this sucks, man. It's just a little cash crunch right now, that's all. I'll pay you bro—I promise."

Boros was steaming and breathing heavy. He let out a barrage of comments for L.D.:

"I don't give a rat's ass 'bout your money problems—"

"This isn't exactly chump change, man—"

"Now listen with both ears—you will pay me and my Boys because—"

"Dude, I'm gonna go ballistic on your ass 'cause—"

L.D., trying to remain calm, replied, "B, B. Chill out, man. I hear you. I'll pay you man. Promise."

"When? When, L.D.?" asked Boros, fuming.

"Friday night—this Friday night."

CHAPTER FIFTY-FIVE

Boudreau, wearing a white apron, was in one of the darkrooms of the DINFOS photojournalism building, a red brick, one-story building that stood directly across the DINFOS classroom building. Boudreau's assigned PJ partner was a short Marine by the name of Mary Nance. She, too, was wearing an apron.

An hour earlier, Boudreau and Nance—like the rest of their classmates—had viewed a forty-five-minute slide presentation on the basics of photography and its contribution to journalism.

"Just like in a news article," the PJ instructor had told the class, "you need to tell a story with your photos. Tell a story with your photos, gang. You know the saying: a picture is worth a thousand words."

Boudreau had taken copious notes during the slide presentation, a slide presentation where he learned:

the importance of light;
the importance of film speed;
the importance of F-stops;
the importance of close-up shots, especially when photographing people;
the importance of no wasted space and "cropping" one's photos;

After the slide presentation, the students had been told to "take photos with your assigned partner and your assigned camera. Switch off and take turns with the camera. Each student should take five photos." Each PJ team was then instructed to develop their film in one of the darkrooms. The PJ instructor, a Navy Petty Officer, had assured each PJ team that "all you need to know about developing film is in the darkroom. Just read the instructions on the walls of the darkroom and read the labels on the canisters." Boudreau and Nance were now in the darkroom developing their film. The only light in the darkroom came from a red bulb that emanated red light.

"Jack, could you pass me the filler container? I need more filler," Mary said. She was an upbeat bubbly sort who spoke fast and smiled often.

"Sure thing," said Boudreau. He was looking at his recently-taken close-up print of a motorcycle parked outside the building's parking lot. He reached up and picked up a container of filler from one of the wooden shelves.

"Here you go, Mary."

"Thanks." A few quiet seconds then, "So, what were your favorite photos in that slide presentation, Jack? Mine was the Ansel Adams shots. The way he photographed those nature scenes, it's just unbelievable."

"Yeah, I liked those too," Boudreau said. He was still looking at his print. "But my favorite has to be the Muhammad Ali/Sonny Liston fight, with Ali standing over his defeated opponent. The photo is so clear—you can see Ali's muscles and his veins. Did you know, Mary, that that fight took place in my home state of Maine? Lewiston, Maine. Famous fight."

"I didn't know that," Mary said. She started pouring filler fluid in a metal tray. "So tell me Jack, how do you like this DINFOS thing so far?"

She turned and smiled at him.

"We're halfway done, you know. Five more weeks to go. Of course, as a Marine, I also have to do the tough broadcasting training here. I'm kinda worried about that."

"So far so good," Boudreau said. "I like this school. And good luck with the broadcasting course. I heard it's tough, but you've got the voice for it."

Inside, Boudreau thought, *Glad I didn't sign up for the Marines or Navy. Ain't no way I'd pass the broadcasting course—not with my voice.*

"Oh thanks, Jack. Thanks for the encouragement," Mary said excitedly. She then said, "Switching gears, Jack, I have a favor to ask you."

"What's that?" he said, keeping an eye on his developing print.

"You know Chuck, right? Chuck Pearson. The tall Marine. He's in your journalism section. Well here's the deal, Jack, I kinda like Chuck. I wanna date him. Can you let him know that I like him and want to date him? And put in a good word for me, Jack."

She batted her eyes at Boudreau. "Yes, put in a good word for me, Jack."

Boudreau thought *This chick's way too excited; way too direct.*

"Uh—yeah. Sure, Mary. I'll let Chuck know."

"Oh, thanks, Jack. Thanks. Thank you, thank you, thank you," she said rapidly. She was all smiles. "You know, Jack, if you would have said something like, 'No Mary, it's better you tell him yourself,' then I would have offered you a blowjob right here, right now. Oh yeah, I would have. Do you doubt that, Jack? Do you believe what I'm telling you?"

Wow, baby. Way too direct.

"Uh no—no, Mary," Boudreau said, his voice a bit shaky. He figured it was best to play along and be agreeable.

"I mean, no, I don't doubt what you said."

He kept looking at his print even though he knew Mary was looking at him. He was uncomfortable.

"Yep, Jack. Right here. I would have taken your apron off, and then you know what would have followed." She was still smiling. "But that won't be necessary because I didn't have to play hard with you. You're easy, Jack. You're cute, too, you know."

* * *

Fifteen minutes later, when he was on a break, Boudreau walked over to Chuck Pearson. Pearson was standing next to a soda machine within the PJ building. He was holding a can of Mountain Dew in his hand.

"Hey, Chuck, got some info for you."

"Hi, Jack. What's up? Whatchaya got for me?"

"My PJ partner's Mary Nance right, and she—"

"Yeah, yeah, I know," Pearson said, cutting off Boudreau in mid-sentence.

He sighed.

"I know Mary, and I know she likes me. She's already asked me out on dates. Shit Jack, I made the mistake of making out with her at one of those weekend hotel parties. Now she's all over me. Mary's cool, but I'm trying to ditch the bitch—know what I mean? I got a girl back home. I ain't interested in Mary Nance."

CHAPTER FIFTY-SIX

The tattooed face of a cat, blue and grinning, covered his right hand; on one shoulder a blue rose blossomed. More markings, self-designed and self executed, ornamented his arms and torso: the head of a dragon with a human skull between its open jaws; bosomy nudes; a gremlin brandishing a pitchfork; the word PEACE accompanied by a cross radiating, in the form of crude strokes, rays of holy light; and two sentimental concoctions – one a bouquet of flowers dedicated to MOTHER-DAD, the other a heart ...

Boy, Capote could sure write thought Boudreau in amazement. *I don't think I've read any better.* In Cold Blood *is truly a classic.* He took his eyes off the page and glanced at his watch.

Three oh eight in the afternoon. Carlos will be here in less than an hour.

He took a sip from his water bottle. The Barnes & Noble bookstore was packed with patrons.

Reading Capote's In Cold Blood, *and reading about tattoos of PEACE makes me think of Boros and the Boys with their tattoos.*

He shifted in his chair and took another sip of water. He started thinking about and reliving that night.

Man, it was just last week. It was a Wednesday night. I remember it was Wednesday, because Wednesday is when we work late at KB Publishers in Lansing to put the Fort Leavenworth Lamp newspaper together. I got off work around seven PM that night, which was early because we normally get off around eight thirty or nine. I drove back to the barracks. I got out of my car, entered the barracks, went to the second floor, and started walking down the blue-carpeted hallway to get to my room, Room 209. There was nothing unusual about hearing the loud rap music in the hallway as I approached my room. I figured my roommate, Boros, and also his buddies, were in the room doing their usual which was drinking beer and smoking cigarettes. My side of the room was fairly private since we had devised a bed sheet to hang between two tall wall closets, thus dividing the room in half. Boros and his Boys never smoked in my half of the room, and they were good about cracking open a window on Boros's side to suck out all that cigarette smoke. Around nine at night was usually when Boros and his Boys would leave the room to do whatever. My side of the room is fairly private, even though it's the side right next to the door. I sure kept a different schedule than Boros did, even if we were roommates. To me, the barracks room is just a place to crash.

I hit the sack between ten and eleven. I often wouldn't hear Boros come in the room later at night. I figure most nights he'd come in around midnight. Some nights he didn't even sleep in our room at all.

But last Wednesday night was different, and I'm thinking it's because I came in early.

Boudreau took another sip of water.

Yeah, it was a timing issue all right. Loud music blasting. I could hear it in the hallway. It was around seven thirty. I entered my room quietly and placed my book bag in the corner next to my bunk. I knew Boros and his Boys were on the other side of the room. I heard a word here and there, but the music was so loud, so I couldn't make out what they were saying. Of course they couldn't see me because we had that divider sheet up. I started to unlace my boots because my plan was to change into my jogging gear. Then, unexpectedly, someone killed the tunes. Someone turned off the boom box or brought the volume down to zero. And then I heard it, man.

"Yeah, fuckin' Scarface paying us late, my Boys. Motherfucker called me earlier tonight and told me he'd pay us Friday instead of tonight. Then he called ten minutes after that and said 'I think I can only pay you half, B.'"

I knew right away it was Boros speaking.

"Fuckin' L.D. Scarface. We make the big shipment for his ass, he owes us the big twenty-five grand, and now he tells us he can't pay on time, and maybe he can only pay us half."

My heart started beating faster. I stood still. Who's Scarface? I thought. Big shipment. Big money. Hell, man, I can put two and two together just like everybody else. Drug trafficking. My roommate's involved in drug trafficking.

I remember the conversation.

"We gotta send the message, my Boys."

"That's right, B. You da man. You da boss."

That was Jackson speaking. I knew his voice too. I remember the whole conversation in that barracks room of mine.

"That's right, I am the boss. Bizzness is bizzness fellas. This drug transport business of ours ain't no Little League."

"That's right, that's right," said Jackson.

Jose and Carlos were back there too, in Boros's section of the room. I heard them occasionally say "fuckin' aye right, B," and shit like that.

"Hey, if I have to use my nine millimeter and pump some lead into L.D's little punk-ass runner's head, then I'll do it. Fuckin' L.D. doesn't do the payment handoffs himself sometimes—he often sends that little punk ass runner of his. If I have to I'll send that little fucker six feet under, man. Make him do some dirt time. That'll send the message to L.D. We need to be paid in full and on time, my Boys. Bizzness is bizzness. Taco Bell parking lot, fellas. This Friday night. I told L.D. he bettah have all the money. I think he will. If not, well, bizzness is bizzness."

"That's right, that's right, boss," Jackson kept saying. "You da man, bro. Send the message, boss. Open up a can of whoop ass if you have to."

That's what was said—something like that anyway. I was hearing all that shit, and there's no way Boros and the Boys heard me enter the room—no way, not with the music that loud. They never would have talked about that stuff if they knew I was in the room. All I kept thinking was "What the fuck do I do? How do I get out of this mess?"

I remember I actually felt my face flush. I know I started sweating too. Thoughts raced through my mind:

Try to exit the room so Boros and the Boys won't know I heard them? That's risky, man—they may hear me open the door, then I'll be screwed.

Stay put and don't make any noise? Maybe the music will kick in again? Who knows, man? That's risky, too. Boros and the Boys often leave this room for piss breaks and shit. And the music hasn't resumed. And Boros and the Boys keep talking.

I didn't know what to do. I was nervous as shit. I knew Boros and the Boys had talked tough around me before, but nothing like this. And I didn't know they were into drug dealing. And who was this L.D. Scarface dude? Me and Boros, man—we were big-time different. Heck, I didn't choose him as a roommate, and he didn't choose me either. I came up on orders to Fort Leavenworth, Kansas, right before the last week of DINFOS, and once I arrived, I of course reported in for inprocessing and the first sergeant told me my assigned room was Room 209 and that "Specialist Boros will be your roommate. He's had a single room now for long enough."

Seconds passed, but I remember it felt like minutes, man. Everything runs in slow-mo when you're mind's racing, at least for me. I kept thinking: "What the hell do I do?" 'Course the whole thing's moot now, and I've got no problem meeting Carlos today. But at that moment, I really was concerned. I just stood there. Frozen. Seconds ticking away. More incriminating talk from Boros and his Boys. And no loud music blasting. I could hear everything. My mind kept spinning for answers, *but in the end, there were only two courses of action: try to exit the room or stay put. The thought of hiding under my bunk also flashed in my mind, but our bunks are so damn low, and then what about my big book bag? I'd have to drag that book bag under the bed too. Plus getting caught hiding under a bunk—that would've given me away.*

Time wasn't on my side either. I figured one of them would have to drain the main vein soon enough. I made my move. I tried to exit the room and go unheard and unnoticed. I did my best to tippy-toe to the door, twist the knob quietly, pick up my big and heavy book bag, and make a quiet exit. That's what I did, man. Luckily I was able to pick up my book bag and at least start opening the door. Then I heard the dreaded, "Jack? You here early."

It was Boros, with a puzzled look all over his face. Sure enough, he had to hit the latrine and he saw me in our room with the door half-way open. I did my best to act calm and stay cool. Again, at least the door was partly open, and I was holding my book bag too. I thought it could look like I had just entered the room.

"Yeah," I remembering telling Boros. "Early night. Newspaper got done early."

He still looked puzzled. Did he know that I had been in the room? That I had heard about his, "Send the message" plans? I think so, but Carlos will tell me, man. Carlos will let me know.

Boudreau looked at his watch.

Carlos will tell me in about forty-five minutes.

CHAPTER FIFTY-SEVEN

"**O**kay DINFOS Student Company. We've taught you guys what you need to know. Now go out and execute."

Tech Sergeant McNeil stood in front of the entire DINFOS Student Company. The meeting was in the same large classroom where nine weeks prior most of the students in attendance had taken the one-hundred question grammar exam. McNeil was standing behind a large podium made of wood. He was his usual excited and passionate self.

"Four days till graduation gang, and the next three of those four days will be your *Final Cut*. Now we've taught you all what you need to know and it's time you put together your own newspaper. Remember, with headlines—no form of *to be*. Dow Breaks 5,000; Cubs edge Pirates in 11 innings; President Clinton to visit India. That's how headlines are written, gang. There's no form of *to be* in them. Remember good leads right off the bat for your articles, and good transitions from paragraph to paragraph. Remember also the inverted-pyramid style of writing—always place the most important facts of your story in the beginning of your news article. Editors, know where to assign your people. Your best photographers should take the photos, your best layout folks should layout your assigned pages, your best writers should write the articles."

Five minutes later, when the assignments were read out loud by McNeil, Boudreau discovered he had been given the job of sports editor for the *Final Cut* newspaper. (Morris was appointed the assistant editor of the entire project, Keller was selected as a features writer, and Smith got placed in the news department). For Boudreau, the job of sports editor was one he had not lobbied for nor desired because he always considered himself more of a worker bee than a manager. And besides, Boudreau couldn't help but remember a popular and oft-quoted saying by his colleagues at his former employer, the *Bangor Daily News*: "Writers can't edit, and editors can't write." Simply put, he never considered himself to be editor material.

After the *Final Cut* assignments came the announcement of the allocated space for each section. Sports was given four pages, and Boudreau, upon hearing of his page quota, quickly met with his assigned staff of six and immediately gave them Fort Benjamin Harrison sporting events to cover. He also assigned Tom Bradley, a Navy sailor, as head photographer, and Sherrie Whitaker, an airman, to be in charge of lay out. Boudreau, like many section editors, pulled two all-nighters during the three days of *Final Cut.*

CHAPTER FIFTY-EIGHT

"**A**re you sure, boss? You think J.B. was in this room when we were talking smack and shit?"

Jackson was standing next to the open window. He had asked the question. It was safe to now ask such a question because Boudreau was gone jogging, and Boros and the Boys knew Boudreau's jogs usually lasted about forty-five minutes. Jose and Carlos, remaining quiet, were sitting on Boros's bunk, while Boros, who had just returned from the restroom, was standing next to the table with the small bowl of popcorn on it. He picked up a kernel and ate it.

"Sure I'm sure," he said, smacking his lips. "It happened just what—less than ten minutes ago. Something gave J.B. away. But that doesn't matter now 'cause I've got a plan, fellas."

"How can you be so sure, boss?" Jackson asked, again having his doubts. "J.B.'s a Boy Scout type, boss. He's a straight arrow. He ain't one to nosey around."

"Like I just said, Jackson, something gave J.B. away, but that's not important."

Boros walked over to the window sill and picked up his already-lit Marlboro Light cigarette. He took a drag.

"Yep, I've gotta plan, fellas." He exhaled the smoke. "Similar thing happened at Fort Campbell and it worked like a charm."

He took another puff and exhaled.

"Jackson my man, as an MP, you'll be important in this. But we'll talk details later, fellas. For now, why don't you dudes split and head to the 2010 Club. I'll meet you guys there in about an hour. For now, lemme just say we're gonna move out of these barracks."

"Move out of the barracks?" Jackson said in wonderment. Jose and Carlos looked at each other, perplexed.

"That's right," said Boros, crushing his cigarette in the ash tray that was next to the popcorn bowl. "We can crash at Dwayne's place in Lansing and pay him rent. Bottom line fellas, Boudreau's gonna get kicked out of the Army. I'm gonna have me a little talk with that straight-arrow Boy Scout when he returns from his jog."

* * *

Boudreau entered his barracks room at eight-thirty. The lights were on in the room so he figured Boros and the Boys were still there. He was sweaty and thirsty from his jog, so he walked over to the small brown mini refrigerator and got himself a bottle of water. He took a gulp. He then walked over to his bunk, grabbed a brown Army towel, and wiped his sweaty face. He was, of course, still bothered by what had transpired in this very room of his some fifty minutes prior, but the jog had done him good, had cleared his head some.

"J.B. buddy, can I see you for a moment?"

It was Boros speaking from his side of the room. Boudreau placed the towel around his neck and walked through the bed-sheet divider. He saw that Boros was alone.

"Well Jack, you're an okay guy and a decent roommate, but me and my Boys are movin' on," Boros said. He was sporting a cocky smile, and his tone was pleasant. "I'll be packing my shit and moving out tomorrow."

"I see," Boudreau said. He wiped some sweat off his face.

"Now, you sure you didn't hear us talking when you came in the room earlier tonight?" Boros asked, still straight forward. "You sure 'bout that?"

There was silence. "Yunno Jack, privacy's important. Everybody needs a bit of quiet private time to talk and shit.

You agree with me right? that people need some privacy to talk 'bout shit."

"Yeah," said Boudreau, growing uncomfortable.

He did his best to act calm.

"I'm telling you, Dustin, I had just entered our room. I hadn't even shut the door completely when I saw you walk through the bed-sheet divider. I had just entered the room when I saw you."

"That's cool, that's cool," Boros said, smiling again. "You know I'm a powerful guy, right? You agree with me that I'm a powerful guy. Ain't that right?"

Boudreau didn't respond. He wasn't sure what to say.

"You see, Jack, I'm one to cross my Ts and dot my Is. I can kick butt and take names later, too. Shit, I can even get someone kicked out of the Army. But we's cool, man, you cool, Jack."

* * *

True to his word, Boros's stuff was all out of the barracks room by the next day, a Thursday, which meant Boudreau had the place to himself.

Sitting on his bunk that Thursday night, Boudreau was nursing a Heineken beer in his right hand.

Man, this is unreal, he thought. He sipped from his beer.

I think Boros knows that I accidentally listened in on their plans. I'm not sure though— it's all weird man. A one-on-one talk with me, something about 'I can even get someone kicked out of the Army.' Then he moves out of this room. Something's up, man—I know it.

He took another sip from his Heineken.

I think something's up. What do I do? See the first sergeant? I don't know, man. Plus maybe this will all go away. Maybe L.D. will pay in full. Christ, man— talk about a 9mm gun and a payment at the Taco Bell parking lot. And fucking Jackson, man. An MP and he's involved in drugs with Boros. Jose and Carlos, too. This is all jacked up.

He finished his beer.

CHAPTER FIFTY-NINE

The DINFOS graduation lasted all of thirty minutes. Airman Riley, a tall, slim, black woman in her late-twenties, had the highest GPA of the class and was thus the class's valedictorian while Morris came in a close second, good for salutatorian bragging rights. Rounding up the class's academic awards was the honor essayist, Petty Officer O'Malley, a short and balding happy-go-lucky type. At the graduation, each graduating student was presented with a certificate, and the Marines and Navy members were reminded "that your ten-week broadcasting training starts later today after lunch."

Boudreau's *Final Cut* sports section had performed well. Together, all sports section members had received the collective grade of ninety. Keller also had performed well academically while Smith, who struggled miserably during features, barely made it through the program.

Standing in their barracks room, their possessions neatly packed in their duffle bags, Boudreau and Keller shook hands and said their goodbyes. It was a warm and sunny September morning. The time was ten in the morning. Boudreau, standing next to his duffle bags, was wearing jeans and a short-sleeve white shirt. In four hours, he had a plane to catch—the itinerary being Indianapolis to Chicago to Boston and finally to Bangor, Maine. Ten days prior, he had come up on orders to Fort Leavenworth, Kansas. His report date to this new duty station of his was ten days away. His game plan was to stuff all his belongings (books, weight bench, cassettes, and clothes) inside his old Volvo and drive from Bangor to Leavenworth, a trek that he figured would take him three days. Keller, standing next to his bunk bed, also had a plane to catch. His was earlier, noon in fact, and his destination was Fort Benning, Georgia. In three days, he would start airborne school. The fact that he was reporting to a military installation later that day explained why he was dressed in his Class A uniform.

"Good luck to you, Jack. Don't get caught doing any funny stuff in Leavenworth because they'll throw you in the slammer right there."

"No worries, Brian. I'll be a good boy." The two shook hands. Keller picked up his two big duffle bags and started heading out the door.

"And good luck with that novel of yours. You started the outline already right?"

"Yeah, yeah, I did. Thanks Brian," said Boudreau. "And thanks for your permanent address—your mom's address in Nevada. I'll write. I'll keep in touch."

"Cool, Jack. Well, my flight's in less than two hours. I better get going. The taxi should be here soon." He then added, "Man, I can't believe how fast these ten weeks went by. It seems like it was just yesterday when I walked into this room and you and Parker were in here."

"Yeah, it sure did go by fast," Boudreau said. "Hey, need help with your bags, Brian?"

"Nah, I'm good, Jack. Thanks." There was a pause, then Keller said, "Hey Jack, about that bet we had. You won, man. I asked Smith today if he ever scored with Morris, and he said he didn't—not with his fiancé visiting him just about every weekend."

"I figured they wouldn't," said Boudreau.

"Yep, well I owe you ten bucks, man."

"Ah, no worries, Brian. Keep your money. Let's make it a gentleman's bet."

* * *

Boudreau's game plan was to get to the airport a bit before noon for his two o'clock flight. To kill time he decided to go to the barracks dayroom and watch some television. He figured he'd do lunch later at the airport.

He was sitting comfortably on the sofa in the dayroom. At first, he was flipping channels, but eventually he settled on *Sports Center* on ESPN. He was all alone, then Morris, wearing blue jeans and a long sleeve collared pink shirt, entered the room.

I can smell her perfume from far away, thought Boudreau as Morris walked toward him. Images of Cindy flashed in his mind. *Cindy always wore good perfume.*

"Hi J.B.," Morris said in her soft voice. She sat next to him. She was smiling.

"Hi Morris. Congrats on being our salutatorian."

Man that's some good perfume.

"Well, I had a great sports editor for *Final Cut*. And call me Paula, please."

"Sure, Paula."

"Well we did it, didn't we, Jack. DINFOS is done. It's been a long ten weeks, wouldn't you say?"

"Yeah, it was a lot of work, but I thought it went by fast though."

"Not me," she said. "I think it dragged on. It was a long ten weeks, but anyway, Jack, my flight's later this afternoon, and I'm still packing. I need some help with a heavy box of mine. Could you help me out? Smith already left with that fiancé of his."

She rolled her eyes. She smiled at Boudreau again.

"Please Jack. It's too heavy for me."

"Sure, Morris," Boudreau said, then she gave him a funny look and he caught himself. "Uh, I mean Paula. Sure Paula."

"Thanks Jack."

Boudreau grabbed the remote and shut the television. Morris, all smiles and confident, grabbed his free hand and led him out of the dayroom.

"This shouldn't take too long now, Jack. Thanks again. I need a guy like you to handle this box."

She kept holding his hand firmly as the two went up the stairs of the barracks building.

"My room's number 201."

Man, her perfume is good, he thought.

"There," she said, still smiling. She placed her room key in the door, unlocked it, and turned on the lights. "Make yourself comfy, Jack."

Boudreau entered the room. His first thought was *this is definitely a girl's room. Everything's neat and clean, and it's got an air-freshener smell to it.* His second thought was, *Morris's luggage bags are in the corner, neat and full. She said she was still packing. And where's this heavy box?*

"Jack, why don't you sit on my bed," she said softly.

Okay he thought.

He said, "Okay."

Morris walked to the window and turned down the blinds. She then opened her purse which was atop a brown mini refrigerator next to her luggage. She fumbled with the purse and got something from it, but Boudreau couldn't see it or make it out. Next to the mini refrigerator was a small desk lamp. Morris turned on the lamp. She looked at Jack. She was smiling again.

"I heard through the grapevine that you and Keller had a little bet going. About me and Smith hooking up."

Boudreau swallowed hard. He sat still on her bunk.

Keller probably told Smith about the bet, then Smith told Morris.

Still smiling, Morris said, "In case you're wondering, Jack, I didn't get any here at DINFOS. Not with Smith. Not with anyone."

She walked next to the door and shut off the lights.

"Desk lamp will do," she said as she turned around and approached him. "Desk lamp will be enough light."

She spoke softly and confidently.

"I like it kinda dark anyway."

She was standing next to him, their knees touching. She took his left hand and guided it to her right breast. She then leaned forward, her movement forcing Boudreau to lie down on her bunk. Boudreau didn't resist—he let himself go.

She was on top of him. She kissed him gently on the lips. Boudreau felt himself respond. She stuck her tongue in his left ear, and she slid her left hand around his crouch. Their eyes met, and they kissed again.

Boudreau thought: *great perfume, and she's got the urge to merge. Sweet.*

She gently took his right hand and placed something in it. It was what she had removed earlier from her purse. Boudreau moved his right fingers to feel what was in his hand. He felt a wrapped condom.

She kissed him again, then she whispered softly in his left ear: "Take me, Jack."

CHAPTER SIXTY

It was a Thursday night. Jackson, an MP, was working the late shift. Boudreau was in his barracks room, sitting on his bunk, sipping Heineken beer. Just the previous evening, he had accidentally heard Boros and his Boys talk about what they'd do if some L.D. Scarface guy didn't pay them in full on Friday night which was tomorrow. Boudreau was all alone in his barracks room because Boros, his roommate, had moved out earlier that day. Boudreau wondered if Boros and the Boys knew he had inadvertently listened in on their plans.

Jackson was on a break during his shift. He was standing outside the Fort Leavenworth Provost Marshal Office, nursing a cigarette. He had his cell phone with him, a cell phone given to him by Boros but paid for by L.D. He punched in Boros's number.

"Boss, it's me —Jackson. Operation Pooch Snoop is a go. Story is it's planned for some time next week. Monday at the earliest."

"Excellent my man, excellent," said Boros.

He, Jose, and Carlos were in the Lansing home of Dwayne Martin, a truck driver and part-time drug runner. All four of them were unpacking boxes because Boros and his Boys were moving in.

"Good work, Jackson. I'll tell Jose and Carlos all about it. They'll do their piece Sunday and Boudreau won't know what hit him."

CHAPTER SIXTY-ONE

Boudreau had arrived at Fort Leavenworth in early September. All his belongings had fit into his old Volvo. The old clunker had needed a new battery but otherwise still ran okay. The trek from Bangor, like he had estimated, had taken three days.

As soon as he arrived, Boudreau reported to his new unit—Headquarters and Headquarters Company, Combined Arms Center—and he met his new first sergeant who promptly told him:

"Specialist Boudreau, you're assigned to Room 209. Boros has had a single for long enough. You two will be roommates." Boudreau moved in, unpacked, and immediately started working as an Army journalist for the Fort Leavenworth *Lamp* newspaper. He had little in common with Boros, but that was okay, especially since the two had such different schedules and hardly ever saw one another.

* * *

About two weeks after Boudreau's arrival, another soldier, fresh out of AIT, got assigned to HHC CAC. His name was Private First Class Greg Kowalski, and he got assigned to Room 217, down the hallway from Boudreau's and Boros's room.

Kowalski, nineteen, had grown up in Reston, Virginia, a suburb of Washington, D.C. He had scored a perfect eight hundred on the math portion of his SATs, the result of which brought him a full scholarship at MIT. The young math whiz, however, promptly turned down the full ride at MIT to piss off his over-demanding father, Alex Kowalski, head of computer programming for an up and coming dot.com. To further piss off his dad, the younger Kowalski had signed up with the Army for three years. His MOS was as a computer programmer (his Dad was at least approving of that), and his game plan was to do the Army thing for those three years, then he'd start his own website developing company. Whenever the elder Kowalski spoke to his only son on the phone, the conversation would inevitably turn to:

"Son, it's a competitive world out there. Education is important. You'll need college," to which the brash nineteen-year-old would respond, "Dad, don't worry. Bill Gates quit college, and look how he turned out. I got this thing all figured out. Website development is gonna take off."

Boudreau and Kowalski would occasionally hang out at coffee shops to discuss politics, books, black jack, movies, and the computer industry. Boudreau was the farthest thing from a techie, but he did follow business news to include the software industry. The young math whiz enjoyed Boudreau's company—he was especially impressed with Boudreau's plans of writing a novel—while Boudreau, for his part, was even more impressed with the nineteen-year-old's abilities, particularly his ability to count cards at the black jack tables. Counting cards at the black jack tables in Kansas City's many casinos was something Kowalski often did for fun and for profit. It was a hobby of his, a hobby that consistently netted him two hundred dollars per week.

CHAPTER SIXTY-TWO

Boudreau was in the Barnes & Noble bookstore reading Capote's *In Cold Blood* :
In the solitary, comfortless course of his recent driftings, Perry had over and over again reviewed this indictment, and had decided it was unjust. He did give a damn—but who had ever given a damn about him? His father? Yes, up to a point. A girl or two— but that was "a long story."

Man, what a great writer Truman Capote was, thought Boudreau. He looked at his watch. It read 3:55.

Carlos will be here shortly.

He closed his copy of *In Cold Blood,* then he reached inside his nearby book bag. He was fumbling for a manila folder inside the bag because that folder was where he kept clipped newspaper articles that interested him, articles from the *Leavenworth Times* or *Kansas City Star* or *Wall Street Journal.* He especially wanted one article for when Carlos showed up.

There he told himself. *My folder,* and just as he placed the folder next to his copy of *In Cold Blood,* he saw Carlos in the bookstore looking for him. He stood up and waved to attract attention. Carlos saw him and headed in Boudreau's direction.

"Hi, Carlos."

"Hi, Jack," Carlos said, taking a seat across the table from Boudreau. He was wearing a black hooded shirt, dark pants, and white sneakers. A Spurs cap, placed off center, hugged his scalp, and his wallet—firmly in his right back pocket—was connected to a short piece of a shiny chain.

"Need anything to drink, Carlos?" asked Boudreau. He was calm. "Soda? Water?"

"Nah, I'm good," said Carlos. He cleared his throat. "Listen Jack, plenty has changed so I'll make it quick. The key thing I wanna tell you is I'm done with the crime thing."

"I see," Boudreau said. The patron traffic had sufficiently diminished so the two were okay talking out loud about such matters, but they still kept their voices low.

"Yeah, finito, my man. No more crime shit for me. By the way, we knew you were in your barracks room and heard us talk about L.D. owing us money."

Boudreau, sensing an opportunity, chimed in with, "Who's L.D. by the way?"

"Drug dealer in Kansas City. It doesn't matter any more though. See Jack, we had the perfect plan to quiet you down."

Boudreau, still calm, said nothing.

"We knew you were in the room. Me, Jose, Jackson—we had our doubts, man, but Boros knew."

Boudreau still said nothing.

Let him talk, he figured.

"It was your boots, Jack. Your boots gave you away."

Boudreau thought back about that Wednesday night. He was drawing a blank.

"My boots?" he said.

"Yeah, bro. See, when Boros saw you inside the room, he noticed the laces of your boots were loose. Later that night, when we were at the 2010 Club, he told us 'why would J.B.'s boots be partially unlaced?' Sure it looked like you had just entered the room, but your laces looked loose as fuck. At least that's what Boros told us. That's how he figured you were in the room for some time and you were actually trying to leave."

I was so focused on my exit strategy, thought Boudreau. *I was also focused on my heavy book bag. Damn—I forgot all about my partially untied laces.*

"Boros wanted you out of the Army, and he wanted you to know he was always a step ahead of you. He figured if you realized you were getting kicked out because of our plan, then you'd keep your mouth shut—that you wouldn't say anything about our drug dealing."

Boudreau quickly thought things over. He figured now was the time to ask "So what was the plan, Carlos? How were you guys planning to get me kicked out of the Army?"

"Too easy, man," said Carlos. "Boros laid it all out for us that night at the 2010 Club. We were gonna place some marijuana joints on top of your room's easy-to-remove foam ceiling tiles. Boros moved out the next day to make sure the room was all yours. Yeah, he turned in his room key, but he made sure he got a copy of it made first so he could go back in your room to plant the joints. He knew a shady locksmith in Kansas City, Kansas, who'll copy anything for the right price. Then Boros tipped the first sergeant and the company commander that there were drugs in the barracks because he had smelled some pot in the hallway. Boros actually told Top that—that he was walking in the hallway and he smelled pot. I'll tell you, Jack, Boros was no dummy."

Boudreau said nothing and kept looking at Carlos.

"Boros correctly figured the company commander would soon order a company-wide urinalysis and a health and welfare inspection—that's what commanders do when they get a tip like that."

Carlos paused for a second to gather his thoughts.

"Shit Jack, the last time our company had a urinalysis was like ten months ago, and a health and welfare inspection was—shit, it was over a year ago. Boros figured a tip like that would definitely get the ball rolling. It sure did, huh? Friggin' inspection and urinalysis was scheduled for the following Monday. Of course, we had Jackson as an MP on the inside. Jackson knew the dudes on the canine team, the MP dudes with the sniffing dogs, and they told Jackson that the piss test and inspection was on for next week sometime. They weren't sure what day, but they knew it was the upcoming week—this past week. We plant the drugs, the inspection takes place, the drug dogs smell the marijuana joints, and boom! Busted. Drug possession. Specialist Boudreau, you're being chaptered out—or maybe even court-martialed—for drug possession. Commanders don't mess with that shit. Soldier possesses drugs, he gets kicked out."

Boudreau remained silent. He noticed Carlos was smiling and excited.

"Jack, do you know how good those dogs can smell? Jackson once told me all about the dogs' drug-sniffing training. They're German Shepherds, and sometimes they've got this other breed. I forget the breed right now."

"Belgian Malinois," Boudreau said confidently. "I should know. I wrote an article about the canine team in the *Lamp* newspaper last month. I know all about the dogs' abilities, Carlos."

Carlos smiled. "Pretty good plan, huh?"

Boudreau had to agree. "Yeah, a good plan. A good plan, Carlos. But how were you guys going to plant the marijuana joints in my room? Boros left the room for good on Thursday. Did he plant the joints right before he left? You guys didn't know when the inspection and the piss test was gonna be till when?"

"That Thursday night. Jackson was on late shift. That's when the canine MPs tipped him off, and told him the inspection and piss test was sometime next week. We called it Operation Pooch Snoop. Anyway, as for planting the drugs, Boros didn't plant the joints when he left because you're right—we didn't know when the inspection would be. Plus believe it or not, we transported drugs, but we didn't smoke the shit. We didn't get the joints till Friday night. Boros figured we had a bit of time to set things up as long as it was before Monday 'cause this 'sometime next week' thing could mean the inspection would be Monday. Anyway, Boros figured the best time to plant the joints in your room was on Sunday. Sunday morning to be exact."

"Sunday?" asked a curious Boudreau.

"Yep, like I told you, Jack, Boros was no dummy. He knew you always went for a jog on Sunday morning. Me, Jose, and Jackson would be in Jose's car in the big parking lot outside the barracks. Once we'd see you exit the barracks to go for your jog, then Jackson would stay in the car with his cell phone. He was our lookout. Me and Jose, also with our cell phones, would enter the barracks. Boros gave us a copy of your room key. Me, I was the hallway lookout. Jose, he was to enter your room and plant the joints on top of your ceiling tiles. It was all planned out well because—"

"Sir, are you Mr. Boudreau?"

Boudreau turned to look behind him. A Barnes & Noble employee was standing next to him.

"Yes ma'am. I'm Mr. Boudreau."

"I have an important call for you in our back office, sir."

"A phone call for me? Who's it from?"

"A Mr. Kowalski or Kawaski—I hope I'm pronouncing that right."

Boudreau stood up and looked at Carlos.

"This will only take a minute."

"No rush, Jack," said Carlos. "Heh, maybe you should get yourself a cell phone some time soon. And say hi to the computer geek for me."

"We'll do."

The Barnes & Noble employee escorted Boudreau to a tiny office behind the cashier's counter.

"What up, Greg? How was Vegas? This must be important."

"Ah Jack, thank God you're still okay. Uh, Vegas—it was a gold mine, buddy. I figured it would be. Made some serious bank, amigo. Pocketed over five grand during my week-long stay."

"That's cool, Greg," said Boudreau. "So, what's up?"

"Well Jack, ten days ago, I bought some high-speed communications equipment at Radio Shack. I didn't get a chance to tell you right then and there, and besides, I only had a day to hook up the stuff because I had the Vegas trip planned.

Paul Bouchard

Anyway, I won't get all into the techie stuff, but the bottom line is I can intercept and listen in on cell phone conversations. I picked up this Operation Pooch Snoop thing from Boros and his crew, and your name popped up, Jack. Something about you not knowing what would hit you—that you'd get kicked out of the Army. I just got back from Vegas, and that's when I listened to the conversations on this answering machine I rigged up. I also heard about what happened over the weekend. I figured you were okay, and I also figured you were at Barnes & Noble, but I thought I'd give you a buzz. Everything cool, Jack?"

"Yeah, everything's fine, Greg. Thanks for calling."

"Great," said Kowalski. "Heh, I'll show you my setup in my room sometime. Nothing illegal, I promise. System really rocks, Jack, lemme tell you. Man, I'm picking up all sorts of traffic. You know Henderson, that hot chick on the third floor. You know who I'm talking about, Jack?"

"Yeah, I know who you're talking about. Henderson. The tall brunette."

"Right. Well get this. Hotty Henderson is having an affair with a Polish Officer attending the Command and General Staff College at Fort Leavenworth. She's pregnant, and the baby's his. She's thinking about getting an abortion. And the Polish Officer—well he's a strict Catholic right, and his wife's here with him. Henderson and the officer go back and forth arguing over shit on their cell phones. The Polish dude's English is sorta broken too. Funny as shit to hear the two of them arguing. He keeps saying: 'Abortion—this is not the proper course of action.' Cool shit, heh?"

"Right Greg. Thanks again for the call. I'll swing by your room sometime tonight or tomorrow."

"Roger buddy. See you then."

Boudreau hung up the phone and returned to the table.

"How's the geek?" asked Carlos.

"Fine. He's fine," said Boudreau.

"Well Jack," said Carlos "you know everything. 'Course the whole thing changed that Saturday night. I knew something was wrong when Jackson and Jose didn't show up Sunday morning to plant the marijuana joints in your room. A fucking tractor-trailer, Jack. Game over."

"Yeah, I know," Boudreau said. "Tragic accident."

He opened the manila folder and pulled out the clipped article.

"It got a lot of press coverage."

He then read the headline to Carlos.

Three GIs Killed in Head-On Collision

Carlos didn't speak.

"Monday morning, Carlos, I went down to the first floor of the barracks to talk things over with Top. I knew you guys' plans about getting paid at the Taco Bell parking lot, and if you guys didn't get paid by the L.D. dude, then Boros said he'd be sending some guy six-feet under. That Sunday night—exactly six days ago—I'm right here at this same bookstore. I take a break from writing, and I decide to read the *Leavenworth Times* Sunday paper. Inside there's this tiniest of articles. It's actually not even an article. It's just a box with a couple of sentences saying, 'A shooting was reported late Friday night. It took place in the parking lot of the Taco Bell in Leavenworth. Anyone with information about this shooting, please contact the Leavenworth Police Department at—' and they listed some phone number. The ad also said 'all callers would remain anonymous.' Here, let me pull out the article."

"Nah, Jack. That won't be necessary," Carlos said. "I know you know your shit."

Boudreau continued. "Well, like I was saying. Monday morning I went down to see the First Sergeant to inform him I knew something 'bout the Taco Bell shooting, but before I could even say a word, Top told me to 'go back to my room,' that there was some inspection scheduled in about ten minutes. Every soldier living in the barracks was called up and told to stay in their room. As you know, Carlos, the inspection took place, and yeah the canine team and the dogs did their sweeps. The urinalysis was later that afternoon."

"Yeah, I know," said Carlos. "We had the perfect plan, but we never got to plant the joints in your room that Sunday morning because the accident was late Saturday night—actually, it was very early Sunday morning, around one AM. Once Boros, Jackson, and Jose were dead, we couldn't plant the joints. I was running around looking for them that Sunday morning, but they never showed up. I found out about the accident from a friend of mine in Kansas City."

Carlos looked down at the floor. He took a deep breath, then he looked at Boudreau.

"I'm done with this whole crime thing, Jack. L.D. still owes us money, but I don't even want my cut."

He looked down at the floor again.

"Once I found out about the accident, I knew right away Jose was the driver. You know, he always had that need for speed. A fucking tractor trailer, Jack. Head on."

"I know," said Boudreau. "The *Leavenworth Times, Kansas City Star*—they both ran articles about the accident on Monday."

"By the way, Jack, in case you're wondering: Boros did shoot L.D.'s runner that Friday night, but he didn't kill him. Dude only had half the money, so Boros told him he'd give him a wake up call. He shot the guy in the leg. Dude sped off right away. I guess someone heard the gun shot and tipped the police about a shooting. Then the cops put an ad in the paper requesting any info."

There was silence. Boudreau's mind started racing.

Good. At least no one died at the shooting.

Maybe I should have seen Top earlier—maybe Thursday or Friday.

Could I have prevented the shooting? I don't know, man. Plus I was thinking maybe Boros and the Boys would be paid in full and—

"You know, Jack, Jose was my best friend," said Carlos. "Damn you, Jose."

Carlos looked up at the ceiling as if he was talking to Carlos in heaven.

"I miss you, amigo."

He did a sign of the cross.

"You know, Jack, me and you are real lucky. I was out with them late Saturday night. We were partying hard because we had some money again, L.D.'s runner had paid us half on Friday night, so we partied hard that Friday night and Saturday night. We were drinking it up and shit, feeling real good that L.D. would get the message and pay us the rest of the twenty-five grand. And of course the next morning—the Sunday morning—we were gonna plant the joints in your room, and Boss figured you getting kicked out of the Army would really seal the deal—that there's no way you'd talk about an earlier shooting. Besides, who would believe a soldier who just got busted for drug possession; who would believe a fuck up who just got kicked out of the Army?"

Carlos paused to gather his thoughts.

"So we had everything covered, and we were partying it up. But I got lucky, man. I was having problems with my girl. We fought that night, and she left Chica's Club early. I ran after her in the parking lot, and we argued some more. That's when I went inside and told Boros I was bringing Maria home, and that I'd crash at her apartment for the night. I remember Boros telling me, 'Okay Carlos. Shit's cool. Take care of the lady. But you know what the game plan is for tomorrow morning, right?' I said sure—that we were planting the joints in your room. So I left early that night. Good thing, man. The only car we had was Jose's. I drove Maria back to her apartment with her car, and I slept at her apartment. The next morning I'm at the barracks, waiting for Jose and Jackson to show up with the marijuana joints, but they never showed up. I'm making all types of calls with my cell phone, trying to figure out where the hell they could be. I found out about that head-on collision later that morning. Shit, Jack, I even saw you leave the barracks for your jog that Sunday morning, and I was thinking: 'where the fuck is Jose and Jackson?' I wasn't worried though—not yet anyway, 'cause I figured we could plant the joints later that day. I figured you'd be out of your room for most of Sunday, either in a place like this or with Greg the computer geek."

Boudreau remained silent. He took a sip of water, then he placed the news clippings in the manila folder.

"Me and you are lucky, Jack. If it weren't for my girlfriend problems, then I too would have died in Jose's car. You Jack, you were lucky by the accident. Anyway, I needed the week to clear my head. That's why I saw you yesterday at your office to see if we could talk."

Carlos paused again, then he said, "Don't worry 'bout me, Jack. I ain't coming after you or anything. No planting of evidence. Tomorrow, Sunday, I leave for San Antonio. Jose's funeral is Monday, two days from now."

Boudreau didn't know what to say. The only thing that came to mind was, *All right, Carlos,* which is what he said. He grabbed the manila folder and placed it in his book bag. He then pulled out a notebook. Carlos stood up and extended his hand.

"We're both lucky, Jack." They shook hands. Carlos turned around and headed out of the bookstore.

CHAPTER SIXTY-THREE

Boudreau opened up his notebook he used to jot down outline notes for his planned novel. He was calm, relaxed, relieved. The talk with Carlos had gone well. He started thinking:

Man, that accident really saved me. The Army is really cracking down on the drug possession thing too. I probably would have been kicked out. And what about Carlos? I think he's genuine. I don't think I need to worry about him, but you never know, man. I'm one to play it safe.

He kept thinking. *There's something—a saying I once heard—that truly represents how I feel right now about the whole Carlos thing,* but he couldn't quite put his finger on it. *What was that saying?*

He remembered it was something that had happened in Basic—something in Basic had triggered the saying, the saying he was now searching for. He decided to look over his outline notes:

Inprocessing week

Basic

Drill and ceremony

Push-ups. Tons of them.

Murdock—Pain is good. Pain is just weakness leaving the body.

Don't be a wuss

Get with the program; drink the fucking Kool Aid

Hard to push the noodle up the flagpole

Y'all ate up like a soup sandwich
This is one big goat rope
Thanks for joining the Army; the juice is worth the squeeze
Chinese Disease = Dragon Ass or Draggin' ass
Motrin = Ranger Candy
Broke dicks
Open mouth and insert foot = shut the fuck up
M16. Sports = slap, pull, observe, release, tap, squeeze
MREs = Meals Rejected by Ethiopians
Lots of hurry up and wait in the Army
"We're all green. No bigots here."
G.I. beans and G.I. gravy. Gee I wish I had joined the Navy
Pukes
Bodette = battle buddy
Blood. Bright red blood makes the green grass grow.
BCGs = Birth Control Glasses
Cadences and PT—remember the cadences because that would be good for novel
Carrington "The Bowler" having to clean up toilet bowls
Carey is Jewish
Carrington is anti-Semitic
Nixon's funeral
M16 Qualification
The Jody letter from Cindy. She ditches me. And I'm still paying for the fucking ring
Tom Lerner, man. Another rooster in the hen house. Ouch!
Grenade throwing—two per soldier
CTT training
Stay alert, stay alive

Suddenly, it hit him. He re-read portions of his outline notes.

Nixon's funeral. Yeah, it was President Nixon's funeral. I remember the drill sergeants gave us the rest of the day off from training because of the state funeral. Our place of duty was in the dayroom and we had to watch the funeral on TV. I remember all the former living presidents were at the funeral along with some other big wigs like Henry Kissinger. I remember looking at my favorite president, President Reagan. Alzheimer's had kicked in so the Great Communicator didn't officially speak at the funeral. But Reagan, man, he was the best. He called it like it was. The Soviets? They're "An Evil Empire." At West Berlin it was "Mr. Gorbachev, tear down this wall!" But my favorite Reagan saying is 'Trust but verify.' 'Trust but verify, man'—that's how I feel about Carlos right now. I trust he just told me the truth, that he's done with the drug dealing, and that he ain't coming after me. But who knows, man? 'Trust but verify.' It's a great saying. I'm gonna verify he won't plant evidence in my room because I'm moving out of the barracks ASAP. Time to get me an apartment—a studio apartment, even renting a room will do. Money's tight, but at least the Bangor landlord let me out of the lease. And I only got one last payment to Kaplan Jewelers on that fucking engagement ring because I've been doubling up and tripling up on those payments. Yeah, it's time for me to move out of the barracks. 'Trust but verify, man.' Never know if Carlos would still plant the drugs in my barracks room. The best way to verify he won't is to move out.

Boudreau stretched his arms and looked up at the ceiling. He was deep in thought.

Man, with what happened last weekend, I think I got myself a novel. Basic, DINFOS, Fort Leavenworth. Boros and the Boys. It's been an interesting ride this Army enlistment thing. Then he thought:

Enlistment – that's my novel title right there. Enlistment.

THE END

GLOSSARY OF TERMS

AIT—Advanced Individual Training. The necessary school military recruits must complete after Basic Training to learn their military jobs otherwise known as MOSs (see Military Occupational Specialty). AIT, which immediately follows Basic Training, is a specific military school where recruits learn their particular military job such as being an infantryman, mechanic, or medic.

At Ease—Drill and ceremony command. When in formation and given the command "At ease" soldiers can relax and chit-chat amongst themselves, but they still must remain standing and in their formation.

AWOL—Absent Without Leave. A punishable offense under the Uniform Code of Military Justice (UCMJ).

Battle Buddy—A soldier helping out a fellow soldier. Teamwork is emphasized in the Army, especially during Basic Training, and tasks are sometimes better accomplished with a battle buddy.

BCGs—An abbreviation for the slang term "birth control glasses." BCGs are Army issued eye glasses that have thick, dark-brown frames. Many soldiers believe BCGs make one look ugly and unattractive to the opposite sex, thus the name.

BDUs—Battle Dress Uniform. The Army camouflage uniform. BDUs consist of a top blouse and trousers. This novel, *Enlistment*, takes place in 1994 when BDUs were the customary Army uniform. BDUs were replaced by ACUs (Army combat uniform) in late 2006.

Bo-lowed—Slang term for failure. Stands for below standards. "I bo-lowed the course." Another military slang term for failure is "washed out," as in "he washed out of the Ranger School."

Broke Dick—A soldier who is constantly hurt or on injured status. The term "broke dick" carries with it a social stigma.

Cluster Fuck—Slang term for "all messed up" as in "this mission is a cluster fuck." Other terms for all messed up include: "ate up," "goat rope," and "ate up like a soup sandwich."

Cadre—Army officers and noncommissioned officers assigned as instructors at military schools. Cadre can include military instructors and drill instructors or drill sergeants.

CTT—Common Tasks Testing. Basic skills every soldier needs to know such as how to read a map, how to administer first aid, and how to don and clear the gas mask. Basic Training recruits are tested on twenty-one CTT skills.

Civilian—Anyone who is not serving in the military. For civilian attire, the word civilian is shortened to civvies as in, "The soldiers wore their civvies today."

GI—Term used to designate members of the military. Stands for "government issue."

Hooah—Military term that can mean almost anything, but commonly refers to "I agree" or "Roger that." The term is pronounced "Who-Ah." It can also be pronounced "Who-Rah."

KP—Kitchen Police. Basic Training recruits are often given work details, and one of them is KP. KP work consists of wiping table tops, mopping floors, and taking out garbage.

MEPS—Military Entrance Processing Station. Facility where prospective military recruits take tests, receive inoculations, get medical physicals, and fill out necessary paperwork to enlist in the military.

MOS—Military Occupational Specialty. One's job in the military, often characterized by a number and a letter. For example, 11B is an infantry soldier, 46Q is an Army print journalist, and a 46R is a broadcast journalist.

NCO—Noncommissioned officer. Army NCOs are soldiers in the ranks of corporal, sergeant, staff sergeant, sergeant first class, master sergeant or first sergeant, and sergeant major. Army commissioned officers have the ranks of second lieutenant, first lieutenant, captain, major, lieutenant colonel, colonel, brigadier general, major general, lieutenant general, and general. Only commissioned officers are referred to as officers. (See next entry).

Officers versus Noncommissioned Officers—Female officers are referred to as "ma'am," and male officers are referred to as "sir." NCOs are referred to as sergeant, except first sergeants are referred to as "first sergeant" or "top," master sergeants are referred to as "master sergeant," and sergeants majors are referred to as "sergeant major." Drill sergeants are referred to as "sergeant" or "drill sergeant."

Parade Rest—A drill and ceremony command. At the position of parade rest, a soldier is standing still and erect, has his feet shoulder width apart, and his hands are placed

228

palms out in the small of his back with his left hand holding the fingers of his right hand.

Position of Attention—Drill and ceremony command. Soldiers at the position of attention stand with their bodies erect, their feet together, their head and eyes to the front, and their arms and hands to the sides just below their hips.

PT—Physical Training. PT can include a series of stretches, exercises, and running. Every Army soldier must pass a PT test twice a year. The Army PT test has three events: two minutes of push-ups, two minutes of sit-ups, and a two-mile run.

Recycled—Not being able to complete a military school during a cycle, thereby having to place that soldier in another class. For example: "Joe failed the summer Basic course and got recycled into the incoming fall class."

Sick Call—Place, usually a medical clinic, where soldiers go to get treatment for an illness.

Smoking—Slang term used to express physical punishment up to the point of near exhaustion as in, "Drill Sergeant Miller ordered me to give him one hundred push-ups—boy, I was smoked," or "he sure smoked me."

0000 to 2400—Military time, based on twenty-four hours, starting and ending at midnight—0100 is one AM, 0020 is two AM, etc.

ABOUT THE AUTHOR

Paul Bouchard is the author of *Enlistment, A Package at Gitmo, The Boy Who Wanted to Be a Man,* and the nonfiction work *A Catholic Marries a Hindu.* He served five years as an Army journalist and is currently a lawyer in the Army JAG Corps. For more on Paul Bouchard visit www.authorpaulbouchard.com.